"Why didn't you tell us the truth about who you are, Mrs. Laine?"

He knew.

Susannah took a breath, trying to think, trying to organize some sort of response. What could she possibly say to Nathan that would make sense of her actions?

"I'm sorry about your husband's death," Nathan said after a moment. "The accident was a terrible thing." His eyes were filled with sympathy. "But it wasn't necessary to hide your identity from us. We wouldn't intrude on your grief." Nathan's deep voice had gone very soft. He put his hand on her shoulder.

Warmth. Comfort. Hot tears stung her eyes. Susannah had an almost uncontrollable urge to step forward, lean against his strong shoulder and let her tears soak his shirt.

She took a deep breath and nodded, trying to swallow tears.

She couldn't give in to that longing to lean on him. She couldn't.

Books by Marta Perry

Love Inspired

A Father's Promise #41
Since You've Been Gone #75
Desperately Seeking Daddy #91
The Doctor Next Door #104
Father Most Blessed #128
A Father's Place #153
†*Hunter's Bride* #172
†*A Mother's Wish* #185
†*A Time To Forgive* #193
†*Promise Forever* #209
Always in Her Heart #220
The Doctor's Christmas #232
True Devotion #241

*Hometown Heroes
†Caldwell Kin

MARTA PERRY

has written everything from Sunday school curriculum to travel articles to magazine stories in twenty years of writing, but she feels she's found her writing home in the stories she writes for Love Inspired.

Marta lives in rural Pennsylvania, but she and her husband spend part of each year at their second home in South Carolina. When she's not writing, she's probably visiting her children and her beautiful grandchildren, traveling or relaxing with a good book. She loves hearing from readers and will be glad to send a signed bookplate on request. She can be reached c/o Steeple Hill Books, 233 Broadway, New York, NY 10279, or visit her on the Web at www.martaperry.com.

TRUE DEVOTION

MARTA PERRY

Love Inspired

Published by Steeple Hill Books™

STEEPLE HILL BOOKS

Steeple
Hill®

ISBN 0-373-87251-8

TRUE DEVOTION

Visit us at www.steeplehill.com

Printed in U.S.A.

Dear friends, let us love one another,
for love comes from God. Everyone who loves
has been born of God and knows God.

—*I John* 4:7

This story is dedicated to my dear sister, Patricia, her husband, Ed, and her beautiful family, with much love.

And, as always, to Brian.

Chapter One

Most people wouldn't throw a pregnant woman out into the cold. But the October sun was warm, and Nathan Sloane wasn't most people. The discovery that his unwanted renter was pregnant just made him more eager to be rid of her.

Nathan stood on the porch of the lakeside cottage, realizing he'd been staring for too long at the auburn-haired woman who'd opened the door to him. He glanced at the registration card in his hand.

"Ms. Morgan?"

She hesitated momentarily. "Yes."

He tried to smile, but the tension that rode him probably made it look more like a grimace. "I'm Nathan Sloane. My father, Daniel, owns Sloane Lodge."

She gave a brief nod, edging the door toward him

slightly, as if ready to close it in his face. "Is something wrong, Mr. Sloane?"

"I'm afraid so." Besides the fact that just being near the cottage rubbed his nerves raw. "My stepsister made an error when she rented the cottage to you."

The woman opened the door a bit wider, letting the autumn sunlight hit her face. It turned her hair to bronze and caught the gold flecks in eyes as deeply green as the hemlocks on the hillside across the lake.

It also showed the purple circles under those eyes, marring her fair skin. She looked like someone who'd been fighting a losing battle with insomnia.

"I don't understand," she said, frowning as if he'd just told her that her credit card had been rejected. "What sort of an error?"

Again he tried the smile. "We're getting ready to winterize the cottages. In fact, my father will be closing the lodge for the season before long." He hoped. "So you see, I'll have to ask you to make other arrangements."

"The person who checked me in earlier didn't say anything about that." She didn't look particularly impressed by the explanation he'd rehearsed.

He spared an irritated thought for his stepsister. "Apparently Jennifer didn't understand. The cottage is not available to rent at all. And certainly not for an entire month at this time of the year."

Her lips tightened. "That's impossible. I've already rented it."

He didn't seem to be getting very far. "Perhaps you'd like to move into the main lodge for a few days until you find something else. Or we'd be glad to call around for alternative accommodations for you."

The woman's fingers were white where they clutched the edge of the door. She released it abruptly. "You'd better come inside."

She walked away from the door, giving him no choice but to follow her. If he clenched his jaw any tighter, it would shatter.

"I'm sorry for the inconvenience..." he began.

"It's more than inconvenient."

The woman stood turned away from him, staring out the windows of the small living room that fronted on the lake. She was so slender that from this angle she didn't even appear to be expecting. Irrationally, he found that made it easier to deal with her.

"I do apologize." He tried to express a warmth he didn't feel.

Get the woman out—that was what he had to do right now. No others were rented. Then he could shut the cottages and persuade his father to close the lodge early for the winter. Maybe by spring he'd have been able to convince his stubborn father that a man who'd narrowly survived one heart attack shouldn't court another by refusing to retire.

Ms. Morgan turned toward him, and for a moment her figure was silhouetted against the windows, her hands pressed against her stomach.

The image hit him like a blow. He saw Linda standing in front of those same windows, head thrown back in laughter as she pressed her hands to her swelling belly.

No. He fought the grief that threatened to overwhelm him. This woman was nothing like Linda. Linda had been gentleness and warmth. This woman was all chilly, sharp edges. He wouldn't let her remind him.

He forced himself to concentrate on her words, shutting out everything else.

"As I said, it's not a question of inconvenience. We have an agreement." Even her smile had an edge to it. "I don't intend to leave."

"An agreement?" He lifted his brows. "I don't recall signing a lease with you, Ms. Morgan."

She didn't look intimidated.

"There's no need for a formal lease in this situation. The person who was operating as your agent checked me in and gave me the keys to this cottage. In my opinion, we have a legally binding agreement."

He suspected his eyebrows went even higher. "You're an attorney."

She wasn't just a nuisance. She was an intelligent nuisance who wouldn't let him gain the slightest advantage.

"As a matter of fact, I am."

He glanced at the address on the registration card in his hand.

"What's a Philadelphia lawyer doing in a place like Lakemont in October?"

Pregnant. And alone, obviously, in spite of the gold band and large matching diamond on her left hand.

"I'm sure Sloane Lodge gets its share of tourists who come to admire the autumn leaves, doesn't it?" She put that hand up to push back a lock of auburn hair that had strayed onto her cheek.

"Leaf peepers generally come on the weekends. And if you'll forgive my saying so, you don't look the type."

She certainly didn't fit his idea of the kind of person who'd settle down in a rustic cottage on a smallish lake in the Pocono Mountains to watch the leaves change colors. Every inch of her, from the burnished auburn hair to the black outfit to the expensive and impractical shoes, shrieked urban professional.

She shrugged. "Let's say I'm looking for quiet and let it go at that."

Too bad he couldn't import a few bulldozers to increase the decibel level.

"Look, Ms. Morgan, surely we can resolve this in a way that suits both of us."

"As far as I'm concerned, this is resolved."

He tried not to look around at the cottage that was

only too familiar to him—living room and kitchen downstairs, with a deck over the lake. Two bedrooms and a bath up the narrow stairs, still decorated in the casual country charm Linda had insisted upon.

And he'd certainly better not think about the master bedroom, with its quilt-covered king-size bed situated to give a view out over the lake immediately on waking.

"This place is too isolated for a pregnant woman alone." The words were like poison on his tongue, and a fierce anger rose in him that she'd pushed him into saying them. "You ought to have someone around."

Her face tightened, the skin drawing bleakly against her high cheekbones. "Frankly, whether I'm alone or not is none of your business. And if you try to evict me because I'm pregnant, you'll be borrowing more trouble than you'll know what to do with."

He'd gone too far, obviously. He tried to tamp down his emotions. "I'm not saying anything of the kind. I'm just asking that you be reasonable."

"Reasonable?" Lightning seemed to spark from her eyes.

His choice of words had been a mistake. He raised his hands, palms outward. "Sorry. I shouldn't have said that. I'd just like to persuade you that you'd be more comfortable elsewhere."

"I'm perfectly comfortable." She rubbed her arms on the sleeves of the loose black sweater she wore, as if chilled, then nodded toward the still-open door. "I am, however, a little tired of this conversation. So if you don't mind..."

Short of removing the woman bodily, he didn't have many options. It was clearly time to beat a strategic retreat. He nodded with as much grace as he could muster and went to the door.

He paused once he reached the porch. "We'll talk again later."

"I won't have changed my mind." The door snapped shut behind him.

He took the two steps off the porch and started down the lane toward the lodge. At least he could breathe again, once he was away from the cottage.

Ms. Susannah Morgan clearly thought she'd won that round. He grimaced. Well, maybe she had.

But that didn't mean he was giving up. For a lot of reasons, he wouldn't be satisfied until he'd convinced Susannah Morgan that she didn't belong here.

Several hours had passed, and Susannah still wasn't sure why she'd reacted so vehemently to Nathan Sloane's presence earlier. She closed the cottage door and stood on the porch for a moment, struggling to zip her jacket.

You're getting bigger, little one. She smoothed her hand over the rounded bulge. *I just wish...*

What did she wish? That she'd taken Sloane's

offer and moved into the lodge, putting off an argument until another day?

There was no real reason she couldn't move into the main building. Her reason for being here required that she stay at Sloane Lodge, but not necessarily in the cottage.

Still, when she'd walked into the cottage, tired and stressed from the trip, a sense of peace had come over her. She'd moved slowly around the small rooms, letting the feeling seep into her very bones, feeling a comfort she hadn't felt in a long time. She didn't want to give that up for Nathan Sloane's arbitrary decision.

She touched the porch railing, noticing the window boxes on the windows and the ladder-back rockers on the tiny porch. Someone had taken a lot of trouble with the cottage. It was a happy place. A place where perhaps, in spite of the disturbing situation that had brought her to Sloane Lodge, she could find the peace that had eluded her for months.

She started up the lane toward the lodge. In spite of Nathan's comments about the cottage being isolated, it really wasn't that far—certainly not more than a quarter of a mile. It would be pleasant to walk on this brisk evening, and the doctor had told her to walk.

Trees spangled with russet and golden leaves lined the lane, but the rounded mountain ridge on the far side of the lake hadn't given up its deep green color yet. Still, the season was turning. What had once seemed like an endless year moved inexorably on. In a month and a half their baby would arrive, another milestone of life without Trevor.

Why did you do it? The question she'd asked so often burst out of hiding again. *Why, Trevor? I know our marriage wasn't perfect, but I did think we were honest with each other. Why did you lie to me about where you were going? Why did you come to this place?*

Any answers Trevor might have given had died with him in the car accident. If she were to find out what had brought Trevor to Sloane Lodge in Lakemont, instead of to the business conference in Boston he'd told her he was attending, she'd have to do it herself.

And she'd have to do it here. If the answers were anywhere, they were at Sloane Lodge.

Only one month. That was all she had before her obstetrician insisted she not travel. One month in which to learn the truth.

The trees gave way to a thick clump of rhododendrons, their glossy leaves hiding the foundation of the lodge. She rounded the building, heading for the door she'd used when she'd gone inside to register. Maybe there was a back entrance from the cottages, but she didn't feel inclined to search for it in the gathering dusk.

The sprawling frame-and-shingle building stretched a wide porch across its front, and welcoming light spilled from the many-paned windows.

She thought again of Nathan Sloane's reaction to her presence. That had been anything but welcoming.

She'd probably see him again at dinner. Bracing herself for the idea of conflict, she mounted the steps and entered the lodge.

Once she was inside the wide front hallway with its bentwood coat racks and curly maple bench, the registration desk lured her. Access to the lodge's records would tell her exactly how long Trevor had stayed before he died and whether that had been his only trip to the lodge. Barren information, probably, but more than she knew now.

But there was no chance to explore. Even now, someone approached from the shadowy rear of the hall.

"You must be Ms. Morgan."

For an instant, before the man stepped into the pool of light from the hall chandelier, she thought the tall figure was Nathan. But this was a much older man, presumably his father. The two men had the same lean, square-jawed face, the same high forehead, the same piercing dark eyes and level brows.

But where Nathan's face was guarded, this man's was open and friendly. Where Nathan's gaze had been antagonistic, his father's radiated welcome.

"Yes, I'm Susannah Morgan." She took the hand he extended, feeling strength and calluses—the hand of a man who worked hard despite his age.

"Daniel Sloane. Welcome to the lodge. Let me show you into the dining room."

Apparently Daniel had no problems with her presence. He didn't seem in the same hurry his son was to close for the winter. He took her arm as gently as if she were made of crystal, guiding her through the archway to the left of the registration desk.

"How lovely."

She paused, glancing from the wall of windows with their view of the lake to the fire that crackled in a massive stone fireplace. Eight or ten round white-linen-covered tables dotted the wide-planked floor. Sloane Lodge might be small, but it was also charming.

"We like it." Her escort looked around, too. His expression was…not pride, exactly. She sought to pin it down. Satisfaction, that was it.

Daniel Sloane looked like a man who had found his place in the world. He was what Nathan might be in thirty years or so, but with an inner peace that shone in his face.

"Now, let's find a seat for you." He moved as if to lead her toward a table where several older couples chatted with the ease of long acquaintance. "I'll introduce you to a few people."

"No. Thank you." She'd have to start talking with people here if she was going to learn anything, but she wasn't quite ready to do that yet. She gave him an apologetic smile. "I'm a bit tired from the drive."

"Of course." He was instantly solicitous. "I get carried away sometimes. Take this table by the window, where you can have a nice, quiet meal." He pulled out a chair for her. "One of the servers will be with you in a moment."

When he'd gone, she looked around cautiously. She'd like to assume Nathan had given up his efforts, but she couldn't quite convince herself of that.

His face loomed in her mind, rigid with determination. He was like the rocky cliff that reared behind the lodge—solid and immovable. Not a man who'd easily give up once he'd decided something. And what he'd decided, unfortunately, was that he wanted her out of here.

Her gaze reached the archway and stopped. Nathan Sloane walked quickly through from the hall. The slightest check in his step when he saw her just confirmed what she already knew. The man had an instant reaction to her, and it certainly wasn't a positive one.

Big, broad shouldered, muscular—he probably often got what he wanted just through the sheer force of his presence. Well, not with her. She faced down worse than Nathan Sloane in Philadelphia courtrooms.

At least, for the moment, he didn't seem to plan on approaching her. He joined his father at a table in the corner, and she let out a small sigh of relief. She really wasn't up to another battle with the man tonight.

She'd been too angry to see it before, but he'd changed. She toyed with her salad, looking back across the years. Nathan wouldn't remember, but she'd met him once before.

She'd been an unhappy ten-year-old, shipped off to stay with Trevor's family for a few weeks at the vacation home they'd owned on the lake. Nathan had been a teenager then, working as a lifeguard at the lake, with no time to notice a pouting child.

Still, through some odd fluke of memory, she could picture him clearly—tall, tanned, laughing and carefree. The center of every group.

He'd changed.

Well, she had, too. Life had a way of doing that to people.

By the time she'd finished her chicken, weariness was taking a firm grip on her. Even Daniel's announcement that dessert and coffee would be served in the lounge couldn't tempt her. She'd planned to slip out quietly and make an early night of it. Tomorrow would be time enough to think of plans.

She'd reached the hallway when she heard a step behind her and felt a light touch on her arm.

"Ms. Morgan."

Morgan. She'd better keep in mind that she'd registered under the maiden name she still used professionally. Given her mother-in-law's tearful opposition to any inquiry into what Trevor had been doing in Lakemont, that precaution had seemed wise.

Besides, if you didn't know what you were going

to find, you'd better tread cautiously. That advice worked both in the courtroom and in life.

She turned slowly to give Nathan an inquiring look, trying not to be intimidated by his frown.

"I hope you've had a chance to reconsider your plans," he said.

He was nothing if not persistent. Annoyingly so. The kind of person who, if you gave an inch, took a mile. If she tried to pacify him by moving into the main lodge, he'd undoubtedly consider it a step toward getting her out entirely.

She pasted a smile on her lips. "There's nothing to reconsider. I'm very comfortable in the cottage."

Daniel came up behind his son just in time to hear her, and he nodded with satisfaction. "Good. We're happy to have you there."

"Really?" She raised her eyebrows. "That wasn't the impression your son gave me."

The flash of anger in Nathan's eyes told her the shot had gone home. She should be ashamed of giving in to the desire to annoy him, but she wasn't. He hadn't had any compunction about harassing her, had he?

Nathan battled to force the anger back under his usual strict control. He wouldn't give Susannah Morgan the satisfaction of knowing she'd gotten under his skin, and he couldn't let his father be upset.

"Nathan?" His father's frowning gaze was troubled and questioning.

"Ms. Morgan misunderstood," he said quickly.

If the woman had any sense at all, she'd heed the warning in his voice. "I was simply concerned about her staying at the cottage alone, that's all."

His father turned to Ms. Morgan with quick concern. "We'd be glad to move you into a room here in the lodge. No trouble at all."

Trouble. Trouble was rushing Dad to the hospital in the middle of the night, not knowing whether the next breath he took would be his last. If he could just get Dad to understand he had to take it easy...

Well, that was a problem for another day. For now, he'd be content with convincing Ms. Morgan to leave his father out of their disagreement.

He focused on the conversation between the two of them, realizing with exasperation that his soft-hearted father was already feeling sorry for Susannah. The next thing he knew, Daniel would be adopting her as another one of his strays.

Look at the way he'd taken Jennifer in without question, even though he wasn't responsible for a stepchild he barely knew. Daniel would keep the lodge open all winter if it meant taking care of one of his lost chicks.

That wasn't going to happen. Determination hardened in him. He'd better detach Ms. Susannah Morgan from his father now.

He summoned up a smile. "Why don't you let me show you around the lodge before you go back to the cottage. I'm sure Jen didn't take the time to do that when you checked in." Before she could think up an argument, he took her arm. "The library is down this hall."

For just an instant he felt her resist. Then she nodded and fell into step with him.

He sensed his father's smiling glance, and he shrugged it off irritably. Dad was too susceptible to anyone he thought needed his protection. Susannah Morgan, in spite of her shadowed eyes and fragile appearance, was well able to stand up for herself.

"This is the library." He led her into the cozy, book-lined room.

She took a step away from him, holding out her hands to the fire burning in the small corner fireplace. "Very nice." She spoke quickly, as if to head off whatever else he might say. "You mentioned Jen. Is she the person who checked me in this afternoon?"

"That's right." He hadn't brought her in here to talk about Jen.

"So you have quite a family operation here, with your sister working the registration desk and your father running the lodge."

"Stepsister," he corrected. "She just helps out after school." And then only when someone stood over her and forced her to.

"Stepsister." She seemed intent on keeping the conversation on Jen, of all people. "Does her mother help with the lodge, as well?"

His jaw felt ready to shatter. "No." He clipped

off the word. "She divorced my father several years ago."

She swung to face him, the firelight burnishing her auburn hair. "I'm sorry." She seemed to assess the oddity of the situation and come to a conclusion. "Your father is a kind person."

"Yes. He is." He gritted his teeth, determined to say whatever was necessary to keep her away from his father. "He's also not well. He barely survived a serious heart attack last winter."

The green eyes he'd been thinking cold and untouchable warmed with emotion. "I'm so sorry. That must have been terrible for both of you."

She reached out toward him. He had no thought of responding to her sympathy, but he found himself taking her hand in his. His gaze locked with hers as their hands met.

The moment seemed to freeze. Nothing moved. Nothing broke the quiet except the crackle of the fire and her quick, indrawn breath.

He shook his head, trying to shake off the feeling. Nothing was happening.

He dropped her hand, clearing his throat. He had to finish what he'd set out to do.

"I hope you can understand why I'm trying to make things easier for him. He never should have opened the lodge at all this season."

If Susannah had been affected by that moment, she didn't show it. She tilted her head to the side, looking at him. "He certainly seems to enjoy what he's doing."

He considered telling her that she knew nothing at all about his father. But he was trying to gain her cooperation, not sabotage his own efforts.

"That's beside the point. He needs to take the time to recuperate."

"Is that what his doctor advises?"

He gritted his teeth. "It's nice of you to be concerned."

"Meaning I should mind my own business?" She lifted perfectly arched brows.

"I didn't say that." He held on to his temper with an effort. "These next couple of weekends will probably be the last for the foliage tourists. After that I'm sure I can convince him to close for the season and get the rest he needs. It's going to be a little hard to do that if we still have a guest."

"I understand your concern for your father." She looked at him for a long moment, as if assessing the truth of his words. He thought he detected sympathy behind the coolness in her eyes. "I don't want to leave, but I will."

Before he could feel relief, she went on. "When the rest of your guests leave, I will, too."

Her expression said he'd have to be content with that.

Chapter Two

Lord, why is this such a struggle? Susannah sat in the wing-backed rocking chair by the cottage window the next day, Bible in her lap, looking out across the lake. *Am I ever going to find peace with Trevor's death?*

No, that wasn't the right question. She fought to be honest in her prayer. She could come to terms with his death. It was the lie she couldn't deal with. Why had Trevor lied to her?

It always came back to that. No matter what else might have been wrong with their marriage, she'd always thought she and Trevor were honest with each other. They'd been friends since childhood. Shouldn't she have known when he'd started lying to her?

Her gaze rested on the familiar passage to which she'd opened the Bible.

"Dear friends, let us love one another, for love comes from God. Everyone who loves has been born of God and knows God."

Not that she needed to read the words. She'd committed them to memory a long time ago. Still, it comforted her to read them now.

She and Trevor had loved one another, though not, she'd begun to see at some point, the way two people united in marriage should love. Maybe they'd both thought they needed someone to belong to. Still, they'd been committed to the vows they'd made before God.

She knew what she had to do. She had to learn the truth about Trevor, so that she could accept it and move on. She and little Sarah Grace could then be a family. They'd be enough for each other.

The baby had been quiet while she'd sat, perhaps soothed by the gentle rocking motion. The chair felt as if it had been put here for just this purpose.

But as she closed the Bible and leaned forward to set it on the convenient lamp table, the baby gave several hard kicks. Susannah patted the spot.

"Take it easy, little one. Everything's all right."

At least, everything would be all right once she'd done what she'd come here to do. And Nathan Sloane's opposition wouldn't stop her.

The memory she'd been holding at bay slid into her mind, and Nathan's frowning face was superimposed on the view of lake and mountain. That moment in the library when they'd touched hands and seemed to touch souls—where had that come from? She knew very little of Nathan, and she didn't like what she did know. She certainly didn't feel any attraction for him.

An accident. That's all it had been. An accidental rush of pregnancy hormones, probably. Nothing more. Still, it might be as well to avoid him, for a number of reasons.

She didn't have to go to Nathan for the answers she needed. Jen could give her access to the registration information, and Daniel, with his kind, observant eyes, might know something of what Trevor had done here, although she'd have to reveal who she was in order to ask.

She stood, hand on the chair arm to steady herself. Pregnancy had affected her balance more than she'd have dreamed it would.

First things first. Today was Saturday, so Jen might be working the registration desk since she wouldn't be in school. She would start there.

When she drove into the parking area at the lodge a few minutes later, she realized that Nathan's comment about leaf watchers arriving on the weekend had been accurate. Cars filled the small lot, and several people in hiking clothes came down the steps as she went up.

The teenage girl she'd met the day before was indeed behind the desk. She wore a sulky expression as she handed a map to an elderly couple, and her black sweater and pants, spiky haircut and dark nail polish seemed designed to announce that she didn't belong here.

Susannah had to hide her smile. No doubt Jen considered her plight unique, and she'd be offended if anyone pointed out that teenagers had been rebelling in the same way for generations.

She waited until the hikers departed, then approached the registration desk. "Hi. I see you're busy working again today."

The girl rolled her eyes in mute protest. "Always. You need something?"

If she wanted to prolong the conversation, she'd better think of something. "I'm going into Lakemont this afternoon. Can you recommend a place for lunch?"

The girl pulled a brochure from a rack and spread it on the counter. With a dark purple nail she tapped the sketch map it contained. "This shows the main drag. Kids say the sandwiches are good at the Fresh Bread Café. I haven't tried them myself."

Susannah lifted her brows questioningly. "You haven't?"

Jen shrugged. "I've only been staying at the lodge a couple weeks." She caught a flash of vulnerability in the girl's heavily mascaraed eyes. "I probably won't be here much longer."

"Going back home, are you?"

As soon as the question was out, she knew she'd made a mistake. Jen's face stiffened, and she shrugged thin shoulders. She shoved the brochure toward Susannah without a word.

This was not going as well as she'd hoped. Jen probably needed a friend, but she obviously didn't consider Susannah a candidate.

"Well, I'll try that café for lunch. Thanks."

"At least you'll get lunch." The girl seemed to give in to the urge to complain. "I've been working on the desk all morning, but does anyone give me a break so I can have something to eat? Oh, no."

Opportunity opened a door, and Susannah stepped through without a second thought. "That's really a shame. I'd be glad to watch the desk for a few minutes so you can run and grab a sandwich."

Jen wavered. "I shouldn't."

"Wouldn't Nathan like it?" She should be ashamed of herself, jumping to the conclusion that Nathan's autocratic ways would be a source of friction.

"Nathan's not the boss of me," Jen flared instantly. She motioned to Susannah to come behind the counter. "Probably nobody will show up while I'm gone, but if they do, the reservations are right here in this file, and guests just sign the book and fill out one of these cards."

It was an old-fashioned register with names and dates. She just needed a few minutes alone to take a look.

Jen rounded the counter, then paused. "You sure you don't mind?"

"Not at all." She had grace enough to feel guilty, but the girl had vanished in an instant through a swinging door at the rear of the hallway.

The hall was still and empty. She couldn't hear anything but a muted clatter of china from somewhere in the back. She wouldn't have a better opportunity than this.

She swiveled the register toward her, noting dates as she flipped the pages back. The lodge had been busy over the summer, less so in the spring. She found the right page. Her stomach clenched as she identified Trevor's neat writing at the bottom of the page.

Nearly a week. He'd been at the lodge for nearly a week, which meant he'd never gone to Boston at all. The faint hope that he'd just stopped at the lodge on the way home from Boston vanished.

She glanced up the page and felt a wave of nausea. There was another entry.

Trevor had been here two weeks earlier than the trip she knew about, for two days that time. Hands shaking, she tried to turn the page back to seek any earlier listings.

"What are you doing?" Nathan's voice, resounding from the stairwell above her, hit her like a blow.

She heard his footsteps approach as her mind scrambled for an explanation, any explanation that might satisfy him. She arranged a smile on her face and turned toward him.

"I was just…" The words died in her throat as she caught sight of Nathan.

A khaki uniform. A dark tie, worn with a badge and official emblem. She read the words emblazoned on the uniform, stomach twisting.

Nathan Sloane was Lakemont's chief of police. The scribbled signature at the bottom of the accident report crystallized in her mind. She hadn't made the connection, and she should have. Nathan was the man who'd investigated Trevor's accident.

Nathan couldn't mistake the expression in Susannah's eyes. He moved slowly to the counter, weighing it. Perfectly innocent people sometimes looked guilty when surprised by a police officer. He wouldn't have thought twice about that.

But Susannah had reflected more than just guilt. She'd been totally dismayed at the sight of him, and he wanted to know why.

"What are you doing?" he repeated.

He could hardly cross-examine one of his father's guests, but he had a right to know why she was behind the registration counter. And why she'd been looking at the guest register. She'd quickly put it down at the sound of his approach, but not before he'd seen her searching through the listings.

"Here, you mean?" She straightened the register, aligning it with the edge of the desk. "Jen hadn't had a chance to get her lunch yet, so I said I'd keep an eye on the desk while she went to get something to eat." Her smile failed to reach her eyes.

Frustration with his stepsister nearly outweighed his curiosity about Susannah. The least Jen could do was help out while she was here.

"Someone would have come to relieve her in a few minutes. She certainly shouldn't have imposed on a guest."

"It's not an imposition. I offered." Susannah started around the counter, the loose russet jacket she wore swinging against her body. "Now that you're here, I suppose you want to take over." She eyed his uniform. "Or are you off to a different job?"

"I do have to go on duty before long." He took a casual step so that he boxed her in between the counter, the stairwell and his body. "I guess you didn't know I'm a police officer."

She'd regained most of her composure, but her hands were still clenched tightly. As if aware of that, she shoved them into her pockets.

"Not just any officer." She nodded toward his insignia. "I see you're the chief of police. I'm impressed."

For the first time, he felt like smiling naturally at her. "Don't be too impressed. In a town like Lakemont, that just means I have two patrolmen and a dispatcher working for me. If any police business actually happens, we all have to get involved."

For some reason, that upped her tension. He could feel it, but he didn't understand.

"I see." She seemed to be talking at random, as

if to cover something else. "I suppose that means you don't spend much time at the lodge."

"I'm here as much as possible. After all, I do live here." He leaned closer, letting that movement intimidate. "I notice you're interested in our guest register."

If he hadn't been so close, he might have missed the way her lips tightened.

She managed an unconvincing smile. "I'm afraid I was just curious as to how busy the lodge is."

Neither of them believed that, but he wasn't ready to contest her statement. Yet.

"Busy enough," he said. "We don't do the business of some of the larger resorts in the Poconos, but Dad likes it that way."

"Speaking of busy, I see Jen is back from lunch." She took advantage of his turning to look to slip past him. "I'm running into town this afternoon, so I'll be on my way."

Someone less suspicious than he was might not have noticed how quickly she scurried toward the front door, as if afraid he might have more questions. Which he did.

He turned back to frown at Jen as she slid behind the counter without looking at him, as if that might make him disappear. He had to deal with his stepsister, but now wasn't the time.

He saw again Susannah's head, coppery in the sunlight slanting through the window, bent over the register. What had the woman been up to?

He went quickly out the front door and stopped at the edge of the drive. Susannah drove past him toward the main road. Those were Pennsylvania plates on her car, and it wasn't a rental. He memorized the number.

Susannah Morgan was hiding something. Whatever her secret was, it had made her uncomfortable with the discovery that he was a cop. It had also prompted her to snoop through the registration log.

He intended to know exactly what that secret was.

"Really, Enid, I'm just fine. Did you help at the charity bazaar this week?"

Susannah held the phone slightly away from her ear while her mother-in-law, distracted, chattered on about the hospital auxiliary bazaar. Enid thought she was visiting with an old college friend, and she had to keep it that way.

Susannah smoothed her hand over the spot where the baby was kicking. She hated lying to Enid, who'd been a part of her life ever since she could remember. But dear, warmhearted Enid had to be protected from anything that might distress her. Her husband and son had always done that, and apparently she was destined to follow the same pattern.

Certainly her mother-in-law would be upset at the knowledge that Susannah had come to the lake to investigate Trevor's lies. Enid refused to believe they were lies. She'd convinced herself that they'd all simply misunderstood.

So here she was, caught in the trap of hiding the truth to make Enid feel better.

"Goodness, I've been talking too long." Enid interrupted herself. "How are you feeling? How's the baby?"

"We're both fine. Don't worry about us."

"Are you having a good time with your friend?"

"Yes, just fine." The knock at the door was a welcome reprieve from expanding on her fable. "I have to go now. I'll call you again in a couple of days."

She hung up, levered herself out of the rocker and went to the door.

"Nathan."

Another person she was lying to. Apparently once she'd started, there was no escape.

He nodded toward the living room. "Do you mind if I come in?"

"Of course not." But she did.

She stood back, holding the door open. Somehow she'd known their conversation earlier hadn't been the end of it. He'd seen her looking at the register, and he wanted to know why. She stiffened to resist him.

He strolled into the living room, glancing around as if to notice any changes. Then he focused on her.

"Did you enjoy your visit to downtown Lakemont today?"

That certainly wasn't the question she'd expected.

He still wore the uniform, and its official aura seemed alien in the cozy room.

She pulled her sweater around her like a protective barrier. "It's charming."

Actually, the village was attractive, although that hadn't been on her mind when she'd walked down the small main street. Instead she'd looked at one shop or restaurant after another.

Were you here, Trevor? Or here? What brought you to Lakemont?

"Did you find what you were looking for?"

He seemed to be reading her mind.

"I wasn't looking for anything in particular. I just wanted to see the town."

She started to turn away from him, but his touch on her arm halted her. Nathan's dark eyes were grave, his mouth firm. Her heart gave an awkward thud.

"Why didn't you tell us the truth about who you are, Mrs. Laine?"

He knew.

She took a breath, trying to think, trying to organize some sort of response. What could she possibly say that would make sense of her actions?

"How did you find out who I am?" Stall. Think of some logical reason for being here other than the real one.

His broad shoulders moved under the uniform shirt. "It wasn't hard."

"Not for a police chief, you mean." She felt a

little spurt of anger. Nathan had used his position to find out who she was.

"I suppose so." His eyes were filled with sympathy. "I'm sorry about your husband's death. The accident was a terrible thing."

Her throat tightened, the anger that had warmed her briefly seeping away. "Yes. It—it was hard to believe."

"I can understand that." Some darkening of his eyes suggested he knew what loss was. "But it wasn't necessary to hide your identity from us. We wouldn't intrude on your grief."

Her mind took a moment to process that, and then she understood. Nathan wasn't wondering what had brought her here. He thought he knew. He thought she had come to assuage her grief, the way people made pilgrimages to the sites of plane crashes.

In a way, perhaps she had, but he couldn't know how complicated it was. And she certainly wouldn't tell him.

"I appreciate that. I just thought it would be simpler if people didn't know who I am. I didn't want to make anyone uncomfortable."

He nodded as if he understood. "Is your mother-in-law planning to come, as well?"

A little flutter of panic went through her. She'd forgotten that Nathan and his family would have known Enid when she'd vacationed at the lake house.

"No, she's not." She had to tell him more than

that. She couldn't risk his deciding for some reason to contact Enid. "Enid has been having a very difficult time adjusting to Trevor's death. She didn't understand why I wanted to come here. In fact, the idea upset her so much that—well, I didn't tell her."

A guarded expression took over from the sympathy in his face. "She doesn't know you're here."

"No. And I'd certainly appreciate it if you'd honor my wishes in this."

For a long moment he just looked at her, eyes grave and assessing. A sudden crazy longing to tell him everything swept over her.

She couldn't. She tamped down the feeling. She hadn't told anyone except Enid, and that only because it had come out in the suddenness of her confusion and grief.

Determination hardened. She owed Trevor her loyalty. Whatever he'd been doing in Lakemont, he'd wanted it kept secret.

Nathan nodded slowly. "All right. I certainly won't say anything, if that's what you want. I'm afraid I've already told my father, though."

"That's fine. I don't really mind who knows here in Lakemont, as long as Enid doesn't find out. She doesn't understand that I—"

Her voice seemed to give out, and hot tears stung her eyes.

"I'm sorry." Nathan's deep voice had gone very soft. He put his hand on her shoulder.

Warmth. Comfort. She had an almost uncontrollable urge to step forward, lean against his strong shoulder and let her tears soak into his shirt.

She took a deep breath and nodded, trying to swallow the tears.

She couldn't give in to that longing to lean on him. She couldn't.

Nathan could feel Susannah's tension and grief through his hand on her shoulder. It seemed to demand a response from him.

He let go abruptly, taking a step away from her. How could he not understand her grief, with the reminders of Linda and everything he had lost all around him?

He gave her a meaningless smile. "We want to do anything we can to make this easier for you."

Something pained and vulnerable crossed her face. She'd reached out to him, and he'd responded with platitudes. That just added to his guilt.

"I appreciate that." Her formal response showed that she'd gotten his message—he didn't want to be involved.

It wasn't Susannah's fault that he resented her presence. She wasn't to blame for the fact that she was the one person in the world whose situation released all the painful memories he'd tried so hard to repress.

Okay. He forced himself to think this situation through rationally. The truth was, he was stuck with the woman. If you were a police chief, part of your responsibility was dealing with people in grief. He'd handled that before. He could handle it now.

And then Susannah would go away and take her reminders with her.

"Do you want to ask me about the accident?"

Survivors did, sometimes, as if understanding how a tragedy had occurred would make it easier to bear.

She shook her head, then cradled her hands across her stomach, seeming to take comfort from the child she was carrying.

"No, I don't have any questions about that. When the police came to tell us, they explained that he'd apparently swerved to avoid a deer and lost control."

"That's right. Several passersby stopped right away to help, but there was nothing they could do."

He shifted his weight, suppressing his longing to get out of there. He had to stay as long as she had questions for him.

But no longer than that. Someone like his father would probably know what to say to ease this for her. He didn't.

The silence stretched, broken only by the tick of the mantel clock.

"Thank you." She managed a smile. "I guess you think my coming here is odd."

"Not really. People often want to see the place where an accident occurred, so they can understand and, well, move on with their healing."

He hoped that sounded comforting. Maybe comfort was the reason she liked the cottage. He couldn't deny the air of comfort it represented.

"You'd prefer I did that healing somewhere else." Her direct gaze challenged him.

"I didn't say that." He'd thought it, but he hadn't said it. "It has been six months, though."

Anger flared in her eyes. "Meaning after six months I should be healed?"

"No, of course not." He hadn't healed after five years. "I just meant that—" He wasn't doing this well at all. "I suppose I'd have expected you to come sooner, if you felt the need to."

The anger faded, leaving her face pale and pinched. "I kept telling myself I didn't need to come here. But eventually I realized that wasn't true. I had to come."

He wasn't one to give advice on this subject, but he had to try. "You have the baby to consider." Maybe if his child had survived—

She crossed her arms around herself, something fierce and maternal in the gesture. "My baby's fine. I wouldn't do anything to endanger her."

Her movement cut him to the heart. He couldn't do this. He couldn't cope with this woman's trouble, not when it held a mirror up to his own.

He retreated a step. "If there's anything I can do, please let me know."

Her face tightened. "Thank you." Her words were formal. "I can handle things on my own."

It was the dismissal he'd been waiting for. He gave a brief nod and went out the door, trying not to act as if he were escaping from something.

Chapter Three

"Go in peace, and may the peace of God go with you."

The minister's benediction echoed through the high-ceilinged sanctuary of the small church and re-sounded in Susannah's heart. Peace. Once again Lakemont seemed to bring her the peace that had been missing in her life for months.

She bent to pick up her coat and handbag from the burgundy pew pad, reluctant to face the probable curiosity of the congregation about the stranger in their midst. But her time here should be easier now that people knew who she was. She could ask questions about Trevor freely.

But she wouldn't be asking any questions of Nathan.

She'd puzzled over his attitude since their conversation the day before, but she still hadn't reached any conclusions. When he'd come into the cottage knowing who she was, he'd seemed sympathetic. But the longer they'd talked, the more edgy he'd become.

Finally it was as if he'd shut down. He'd been unable to relate to her any longer.

Some people were made uncomfortable by others' grief. It could be that, but she didn't quite believe the answer was that simple. She'd sensed some strong emotion moving behind his solid exterior. Whatever that feeling had been, he clearly hadn't meant to share it with her.

She moved into the aisle, grasping the carved arm of the pew for balance. Her nerves came to attention. Nathan was just a few people ahead of her. He held his father's arm, and a sulky Jen trailed behind them.

Nathan in a suit and tie might have looked oddly formal, since the man seemed to prefer jeans when he wasn't in uniform, but that wasn't the impression she got. His assured stance didn't change no matter what he wore.

The line of people worked its way slowly back down the aisle toward the door. Everyone in the small sanctuary seemed determined to be friendly. Susannah had to stop every few feet to respond to introductions and welcoming words. She evaded invitations to come again and tried not to be aware that Nathan could probably hear every word she said.

What difference did that make? She wasn't trying to impress Nathan Sloane.

Maybe not, but she couldn't ignore him, either.

She reached the door at last and shook hands with the young pastor. When she stepped out into the sunshine, she found that the party from the lodge was waiting for her. Daniel came forward, hand outstretched.

"Glad you joined us at worship, Susannah. If we'd known you were coming, you could have ridden with us."

The older man's open, welcoming smile was a marked contrast to Nathan's closed and shuttered expression. And to Jen's totally bored look, for that matter.

"That's kind of you. It was a lovely service. Your congregation is certainly friendly." Except, possibly, for one member.

"We try to be." Daniel, apparently feeling his son's silence to be oppressive, gave him a sharp look. "You might like to join us for the potluck supper we're having on Wednesday evening. You'd be more than welcome, and you don't have to bring anything."

Nathan shifted his weight from one foot to the other, as if eager to get moving. "I doubt Susannah's interested in getting that involved with the church. Not that you're not welcome," he added, apparently feeling he'd sounded eager to be rid of her.

Which he was, as far as she could tell. She'd like to know why.

"Thank you. I'll see how things are going by Wednesday." She took a step away from them. "I think I'll take a walk through town, as long as I'm here."

"You know, maybe I'll join you," Daniel said.

"I thought you were going to relax and read the paper after church." Nathan's tone clearly conveyed disapproval.

"Later." Daniel nodded cheerfully to his son. "You go ahead and take Jen home. I'll ride back with Susannah." He glanced at her with a smile. "If that's all right with you."

"I'd be happy for the company."

She ignored Nathan's frown. Daniel wouldn't be maneuvering to be alone in her company unless he had something to say that he didn't want the others to hear. Her pulse quickened. Something about Trevor's visits to Lakemont?

Without waiting for any further response from his son, Daniel took her arm. He steered her away, leaving the other two looking after them.

The sidewalk led along the lakefront, with shops and restaurants lining the opposite side of the narrow street. Susannah looked out over the lake, seeing the gold and red of the turning leaves reflected in its mirrored surface.

"It's a gorgeous day for a walk." She glanced at the man next to her as Daniel matched his stride to hers. Remembering what Nathan had said about his heart attack, she slowed down a little.

"It is that."

"But I have the feeling there's something on your mind besides taking a stroll."

His smile was very like Nathan's. "Oh, I don't know. A walk seemed like a good idea. My son's too inclined to fuss over me."

"He worries about you because he loves you. That's a good thing."

"It is." His eyes twinkled. "Just a little irksome at times."

"I suppose so." She thought of her own efforts to escape Enid's constant pampering. "My mother-in-law tends to do that to me."

"Well, yes, Enid always did flutter, as I recall. I can understand why you don't want her to know you're here."

They'd edged into the topic on her mind, and she tried to find a way to ask her questions. Maybe the only way was to come right out with it.

She stopped, hand on the railing that lined the walk. Daniel halted next her, leaning on the rail. A little farther along an intent young man focused his camera on the view of lake and mountains.

"Do you remember much about Trevor's stay at the lodge in the spring?"

"Sure I do. It was a pleasure to see that boy again." He shook his head, smiling. "I don't suppose he'd have appreciated my calling him a boy, but that's how I remember him. Trevor wasn't a man yet when the family stopped coming here in the summer.''

''The vacation house burned down, didn't it? I suppose that's why they didn't come back.''

''I guess that was it. Anyway, it was nice to see Trevor again.''

''What did he do while he was here?'' She hesitated, wondering if she should try to explain that question in some way, but Daniel didn't seem to think it odd.

''Well, I'm not sure I know exactly. He went into town most evenings, as I recall. Oh, and I know he went to the ruins of the old house.''

She frowned, trying to remember the last time Trevor had mentioned the vacation house. ''Did he say why he wanted to see it?''

He shrugged. ''Sentiment, I suppose. Or maybe he was thinking about rebuilding.''

''Maybe.'' He'd have talked to Enid about that, surely.

She tried to picture Trevor walking around Lakemont in the evenings, tried to imagine him visiting the ruins of the place where he'd spent summers as a boy.

It didn't seem to help much, but at least it gave her a place to start. She'd pay her own visit to whatever remained of the summerhouse.

Daniel patted her hand. ''If you want to talk about him anytime, I'm here. We'd all like to help you.''

All but Nathan.

"I'm afraid I make your son uncomfortable." The words were out before she considered that they might sound critical.

"Well, Nathan's got his own set of problems." He glanced at her, the look questioning. "You know about his wife, don't you?"

"I didn't know he was married."

He nodded. "Married his high school sweetheart. He and Linda never seemed to have eyes for anyone else. She died five years ago."

Shock jolted her, and she clung to the railing, the wood rough on her palm. "I'm so sorry. I didn't realize." No wonder Nathan was edgy around her. "I suppose my being here, my grief, reminds him of his own loss."

"Well, it's not just that." Daniel hesitated, the lines in his face deepening. He seemed reluctant to say something he knew he must. "The thing is, Nathan and Linda lived in the cottage you're staying in. And she was pregnant when she died."

The words hit her like a blow. For a moment she couldn't breathe, couldn't even think.

Poor Nathan. No wonder he hated being in the cottage with her. Hated seeing her there.

"I—" She didn't know what to say first. "I'm sorry," she said again. "Why did Jen put me in the cottage?"

"She didn't know about Linda." He shrugged.

"And we do rent the cottage when someone wants it. It's just unfortunate that—"

"That it happened to be me." She shook her head, feeling a little nauseated. "How did his wife die? What happened to her?"

Sorrow carved deeper lines in his face. "The doctors said Linda had an undetected heart defect. One of those things that people never even know they have." He paused. "It wasn't anyone's fault, but she and the baby both died."

She rubbed her arms, trying to ward off the chill that settled into her bones. Or her heart. No wonder Nathan was so protective of his father after his heart attack.

"Should I move out of the cottage?"

Daniel's gaze was troubled. "I thought so at first. But it seems as if having you there is making Nathan face his feelings instead of locking them away. That might be a good thing."

"I can move into the lodge." Her preference for the cottage paled in the face of this information.

"If you're okay with it, maybe you ought to stay where you are. Maybe it's better that way." He put the words cautiously, as if he thought she might be upset at knowing the pregnant woman who'd lived there had died.

She was upset, but not out of any superstitious fear.

"All right. I'll stay at the cottage for now, but if you change your mind, just let me know."

He nodded, his face still troubled.

Poor Nathan.

The words repeated themselves in her mind. Was that what people were saying about her? She found she didn't like the sound of it.

She understood. Of all the people in the world, she understood what Nathan was feeling.

That sense of intimate knowledge shook her. It might be better not to empathize so well. It might be safer for both of them.

Susannah had come to the lodge for breakfast the next morning because she couldn't face staying alone at the cottage any longer. But even an excellent breakfast hadn't dispelled the cloud that hung over her.

The dining room had emptied gradually. She was left alone with the server who was clearing tables.

She couldn't dismiss Daniel's words from her mind. Nathan's young wife, and his child, wiped out of his life in a moment.

And how she was going to face Nathan again with this knowledge hovering in her consciousness— well, maybe it would be better if she didn't see him for a while.

"More tea, Ms. Laine?" The server hovered over her, teapot at the ready. *Laine.* She'd given up the pretence once Nathan and his father knew the truth. She'd probably stand a better chance of finding something out this way, in any case.

"No, thanks, Rhoda."

The woman nodded, returning the teapot to her tray and removing Susannah's dishes deftly. Rhoda Welsh apparently did just about everything at the lodge. She was quick and efficient, and she certainly didn't chatter. In fact, Susannah hadn't seen her exchange more than a couple of words with anyone.

Susannah watched her idly. She was in her late thirties probably, with a fine-boned, impassive face that didn't give anything away. She'd be an attractive woman if she weren't so withdrawn.

"It's quiet after the weekend, isn't it?"

Rhoda looked startled to have a response expected of her. "I suppose so." She set dishes on the tray. "Would you like anything else?"

The woman's bland politeness seemed to repel further comment. The impulse Susannah had had to ask if she remembered Trevor withered away. What could the woman say, even if she bothered to answer?

"No, that's all. Thank you."

The woman slipped noiselessly away. Susannah picked up her jacket and bag and crossed the dining room. At least she had a destination in mind this morning.

As she pushed open the door, Nathan jogged up the stairs toward her. In fact, *jogged* did seem to be the operative word. Perspiration beaded on his forehead, and his dark hair clung damply to his head.

He wore sweats and sneakers, and he'd obviously been running.

He held the door for her. "Good morning. Where are you off to this morning?"

He was trying to be pleasant, and that had to cost him an effort.

"I'm planning to have a look at what's left of the vacation house." *Because your father told me yesterday that Trevor did that when he was here.* "I suppose Enid and I really ought to do something about the property."

He frowned. "You can't do that."

She lifted her eyebrows. "I beg your pardon?"

He planted a large hand on the porch post, as if to bar her way. "I mean, you shouldn't go over there. Not alone. The place is an overgrown mess."

"All the more reason why I should have a look." She brushed past him and started down the steps.

He followed her. "Look, I'm telling you, it's not safe. They never did a proper job of razing the house. You shouldn't be wandering around there—"

"Alone," she finished for him, her voice tart. "I know. I get the message. I'll be careful." She started toward her car.

He caught her arm, turned her so that she faced the police cruiser, and opened the door.

She impaled him with her coolest stare. "Are you arresting me?"

"No, I'm taking you to the Laine house." At her incredulous expression, he gave an exasperated sigh.

"If you're that determined to go, I'll take you. I don't want to have it on my conscience if you fall down and break an ankle. Can you wait until I shower?" He swung the towel from around his neck and wiped his face.

"I don't need your help." Well, that sounded petulant. She tried again. "I appreciate your offer, but I'll be perfectly fine by myself."

"Look, if you're going, I'm going with you, so you may as well get in the car and save us both an argument."

His face looked as if it had been carved from the same rock as the cliff above them. Clearly he didn't intend to give an inch. If she drove alone, he'd probably follow her.

She slid into the front seat of the cruiser. With a nod that accepted her capitulation, he closed the door.

He got in and started the car while she surveyed the dash with its police radio.

"I've never been in a police cruiser before. It's intimidating."

His lips twitched. "You haven't seemed too intimidated so far. Exactly the opposite, as a matter of fact."

"That's just because you're overprotective. Ordinarily I'm perfectly agreeable."

Fifteen minutes ago she'd been worrying about how she'd face him. Now they seemed to have reached a new level of communication, and she wasn't sure why. Because she'd forgotten about his history while they were busy arguing?

Maybe. Or maybe he'd forced his way past the reminder she represented of his own grief.

Whatever had caused it, she could only be grateful. She didn't want to walk on eggshells around Nathan for the rest of her stay. She settled back against the seat as the cruiser pulled out of the parking area.

The road wound along the lake, a gray ribbon unfurling through a patchwork of gold, green and red. The maples were already dropping their leaves, and the sumacs sent red spires toward the sky like so many torches.

"Beautiful, isn't it?" She glanced toward him, to find him frowning at the road ahead.

"What? Oh, sure." Clearly he hadn't been thinking about the scenery.

Was he thinking about what a nuisance she was? Or speculating on how soon she'd be out of his hair?

A wave of annoyance went through her. "Look, you really didn't have to do this."

Nathan didn't look at her, but his eyebrow rose slightly. "I thought we were finished with that conversation." He slowed, flicking the turn signal. "We're here, anyway."

He turned into the lane. She remembered the road as wide and well kept, but now it was a rutted, overgrown trail through a tangle of undergrowth. She probably wouldn't have been able to pick out the turnoff if she'd been alone.

"I see what you meant about the place." She winced as a dangling crimson vine of Virginia creeper slapped the car's windshield. "Maybe this isn't such a good idea. I wouldn't want to be responsible for damage to the police cruiser."

"It's been through worse." He steered around a deep pothole and rounded a clump of rhododendron.

They emerged into the open by the water. Nathan stopped the car where the lane petered out. He leaned across her to gesture to the right.

"That's all that's left, I'm afraid."

She remembered a gracious clapboard house with a wide porch overlooking the lake. Now blackened timbers jutted upward, and a tangled mass of wrought iron sagged to the ground where the porch had been.

She unbuckled her seat belt and slid out without waiting for Nathan to help her. She stood looking, trying to imagine what the fire must have been like.

She swallowed hard, saddened at the devastation. "Depressing, isn't it?"

He came around the car to stand next to her. "I'm afraid by the time the fire trucks got here, it was past saving. That happens too often with vacant cottages. I always wondered why Trevor's parents didn't either rebuild the house or sell the land."

That would have been her late father-in-law's decision. He'd always decided everything, while Enid smiled and nodded agreement.

"Trevor came over when he was here." She repeated what Daniel had said, trying to make sense of that visit.

Nathan nodded. "I remember he mentioned wanting to see the place. Was he planning to rebuild?"

That was obviously something she should have known if she'd been aware of Trevor's visit to the lodge.

"I don't think he'd decided yet." She leaned back against the car, absorbing its warmth. A ray of sunlight, striking through crimson leaves, gave the illusion the fire still burned. "I remember how much he loved this place when he was a kid."

He leaned against the car, next to her, apparently content to let her take as long as she wanted. "Had you ever been here with him?"

"Not after we were married. I was here as a child, though."

He turned to look at her. "You were? I guess that means you knew Trevor for a long time."

"Our mothers were close friends, so we grew up together. I came to the lake for a visit when I was ten."

"Did you enjoy yourself?"

She pressed her palms against the car as that visit came to life in her memory. "It wasn't a happy time for me. My mother was in the hospital, and my father sent me to Enid while she had surgery."

"That's hard on a kid. You must have been scared." His voice warmed with sympathy.

"Scared, mad, you name it. You know what it's like when you sense that something's terribly wrong and no one will tell you the truth?"

He seemed to understand what she didn't say. "Your mother?"

"It was cancer. She didn't make it."

She wouldn't tell him the rest of it—that her father, always dependent on her mother's strength, hadn't known what to do with her after her mother's death. That she'd spent most of her time after that at boarding school or farmed out to friends, her home life gone.

She moved her hand to her stomach. *That's not going to happen to you, little Sarah.*

"I'm so sorry." His shoulder pressed warmly against hers. "That was rough."

Her throat tightened, and again she felt that irrational longing to lean against him. But she couldn't. It was time to lighten this conversation.

"Be sorry for everyone around me that summer. I made their lives miserable, too."

"They could probably take it."

She glanced at him. He had a cleft in his chin that seemed to mitigate his face's stern planes. "Actually, I remember a certain lifeguard telling me to stop being a brat."

"Me?" He raised those level brows. "I'd never

have said that to a kid. You must be thinking of someone else.''

"No, it was you, all right. Nathan Sloane, the most popular guy on the beach. All the teenage girls vied for your attention. It's a wonder one of them didn't try drowning herself to get it.''

He grinned, his face relaxing. "Actually, I did hear a few phony calls for help in my time.''

His smile did amazing things to his usually serious face. No wonder the girls had been crazy about him.

"I also remember seeing you hanging around the baby-sitter Enid had for Trevor and me. In fact, I caught you kissing her one night right down there on the dock.''

She gestured toward the spot, then turned back toward him. Her heart jolted. The smile had been wiped from his face, leaving it stripped and hard.

Then she remembered. Linda. The baby-sitter had been Linda Everett. The woman he married. The woman he'd lost.

Chapter Four

Sitting on the front porch of the cottage the next afternoon, Susannah watched as the police cruiser pulled out of the lodge's parking lot and disappeared toward town in a swirl of autumn leaves. Nathan had gone. It was safe to go to the lodge.

Safe? She thought about the word. Who was she trying to protect—Nathan or herself?

Those moments at the ruined house were permanently engraved upon her mind. She'd been careless, and her unthinking words had hurt him.

She pressed her hand against the spot where the baby seemed to be doing gymnastics. She certainly hadn't intended to cause him pain with her mention of that long-ago summer. She'd actually been relieved because they'd seemed able to converse like any two casual acquaintances.

Well, clearly they couldn't. Her very presence

was a constant irritation to him, and she had to accept that. The best thing she could do for herself and for Nathan was to avoid him entirely.

She shoved herself out of the rocking chair, holding the porch post for a moment for balance. Their visit to the old summerhouse hadn't accomplished anything except to put another barrier between her and Nathan.

She'd have to find out some other way what had taken Trevor there. She descended the steps and started toward the lodge. She'd talk with Daniel again. Maybe he'd remember something else Trevor had said.

A small voice whispered in her mind that she was avoiding the obvious. Enid might know why Trevor would want to see the ruins of their vacation home.

But Enid was out of bounds at the moment, because Enid didn't know what she was up to. Questioning her would only raise suspicions, in addition to a flood of tears. No, it was better this way.

She entered the lodge, blinking as her eyes adjusted to the dimness after the brilliant display of color outside. Daniel was behind the registration desk, as she'd hoped. But he wasn't alone.

"I'd think you'd want me to work on this stupid homecoming float." Jen leaned toward Daniel, every line of her slight figure tense in her black jeans and sweater. "You're always telling me to get involved in stuff."

"Of course I want you to participate." Daniel's

usually serene face looked ruffled. "But you know I don't understand this computer. If I try to do these entries, goodness knows where they'll end up."

That sounded remarkably like an invitation to Susannah. "May I help you with that?"

Their faces swung toward her, startled, and she realized they'd been so engrossed in their own battle that they hadn't known she was there.

"I couldn't help but overhear." She put an apology in her tone as she moved toward the desk. "If you're having trouble with the computer, maybe I can help."

"We couldn't ask you to do that," Daniel said. "You're a guest."

"It's just a couple of entries," the girl put in quickly. "Rhoda will give me a ride to town, but I have to go now."

"Sure thing." Susannah slipped off her jacket. "I'd be glad to help—" She almost said, "your father," but stopped herself in time.

Daniel was Jen's stepfather, which made her presence at the lodge odd. Why was she with Daniel, when her mother had divorced him? It wasn't any of her business, of course, but she couldn't help wondering.

Fortunately neither of them seemed to notice her hesitation. "Okay, great." Jen dashed toward the door. Rhoda must be waiting in the parking lot.

"Thank you." The words floated back over her shoulder as the door banged.

The girl's actions brought a smile to Susannah's face. She remembered that feeling—that adults were merely obstacles to be overcome on the way to her real life with her peers.

"I'm sorry." Daniel spread his hands. "I'll take care of these entries somehow. It's just that Nathan said—"

He stopped, but Susannah thought she could fill in the rest of the sentence. Nathan had probably said that Jen should do a little more to pull her weight at the lodge.

"Please, let me help." She moved behind the counter before he could object. She wanted a private conversation with Daniel, and it had fallen into her lap. "Show me what you're struggling with."

"You'll think I'm pretty stupid not to be able to figure this out myself. I'm sure Jen does."

She couldn't quite decipher the emotion behind that last sentence. Regret, maybe?

"Teenagers think anyone over thirty is hopelessly behind the times." She took his place in front of the computer.

"That's me, all right."

Susannah moved the mouse, and the screen saver disappeared, to be replaced by a spreadsheet. "Were you entering these?" She nodded toward a page of names and addresses next to the computer.

Daniel nodded. "But you shouldn't bother. You're a guest."

She picked up the list. "Please. You're an old friend of my husband's family, aren't you?"

He smiled. "It does feel as if we should already be friends. After all, I knew Trevor from the time he was just a little tyke."

Susannah focused her gaze on the screen as she began inputting the data, but all her attention was on him. "I suppose you and he talked about old times when he was here that last time." She tried to say it casually, as if it didn't matter to her.

"Not too much, actually. Trevor seemed distracted, as if he had something on his mind."

She looked at him. "What makes you say that?"

Daniel shifted, as if the direct question made him uncomfortable. "Oh, I don't know. He'd sit at the table in the library, where there's a computer hookup, and work on his laptop."

That laptop might have provided some information, but it had been destroyed in the accident.

"Catching up on work, maybe," she suggested.

"Sometimes he'd just be looking off into space," Daniel said. He shrugged. "I guess that doesn't amount to much, really."

No, she supposed not. Trevor could have been concentrating on some new business project. But if that were the case, why would he have lied about where he was going?

Daniel's expression had turned worried, probably at her silence, and she managed to smile at him.

"I imagine he was thinking about the business. He found it hard to leave behind."

"Guess so." Daniel nodded. "Let me get you a cup of herbal tea while you're working." He started through the archway into the dining room, then paused, half turning back toward her. "You know, there was one other thing that made me think Trevor had something on his mind."

"What was that?" Her stomach clenched as if it knew something bad was coming.

"He asked me about Pastor Winstead—what he was like, could he be discreet, that kind of thing. Then he made an appointment to go and talk with him."

Fortunately Daniel didn't seem to expect a response to that. He disappeared toward the kitchen.

A wave of nausea swept over Susannah, and she stood very still until it abated. Most people would add all these facts together and come up with a man who was distressed about his marriage, having an affair, or both.

Everything in her rejected that. Trevor had been an honorable man. He wouldn't…

But he had lied. What else was big enough to make an otherwise honorable man lie?

A step sounded in the hall behind her.

"I know I've said this before, but what are you doing back there?" Nathan stopped, looked more closely at her face and then quickly rounded the desk to stand next to her. "What's wrong?"

''Nothing.'' He was too close in the small space behind the registration desk, and she was way too aware of the solid masculine strength of him.

He clasped her arm and lowered her to the closest chair. ''Then why do you look as if you're about to faint?''

Because I think my husband was unfaithful.

No. She wouldn't say that.

''I wasn't about to faint. I'm perfectly fine.'' She met his frowning gaze with a frown of her own. ''I thought you'd gone to work.''

He lifted an eyebrow. ''Why did you think that?''

At least he hadn't asked why it mattered to her. That was the question she didn't want to answer.

''I happened to see the police cruiser pull out earlier, that's all.''

He was still standing too close, his hand resting on the back of the chair, brushing her shoulder. Ridiculous to feel a wave of warmth coming from that hand.

''Let's go back to my original question, then. What are you doing here?'' A jerk of his head took in the registration area and the computer. ''Did I imagine it, or did I actually see you entering something on the computer?''

''It's no big deal.'' She mentally deleted any reference to Jen. ''Your father was having an argument with the computer when I came in, so I offered to help him out.''

Nathan's jaw tensed, a small muscle at the corner

of his mouth twitching, probably with annoyance. "He wasn't supposed to be doing that at all. And you certainly shouldn't take it on. It's Jen's job."

Apparently it was impossible to avoid the subject of his stepsister. "What difference does it make, as long as it gets done?"

"Jen—"

"Jen was, as I understand, getting a ride to town to work on the church youth group's homecoming float. That's a worthwhile project, surely."

His look combined that characteristic stubbornness with his obvious opinion that his stepsister's activities were none of her business. "She still shouldn't have dumped the work on you. You're a guest."

"A guest with too much time on her hands. I was happy to find something to keep me busy." She looked up at him. "And we are old friends, aren't we?"

If that reminded him of her careless words yesterday, he didn't show it. He just nodded, perhaps reluctantly. "I guess so. But you still shouldn't—"

She put her hand over his to stop him, then wished she hadn't. There was entirely too much magnetism in the man to make touching him a safe thing to do.

Safe. There was that word again. It did seem to crop up where Nathan was concerned.

"Look, your father wanted Jen to go. He wants

her to have something that will make her feel as if she belongs here.''

His hand turned, clasping hers in a strong grip that made its warmth felt clear up her arm. ''You're a nice person, Susannah. But I'm afraid it will take more than the youth group float to make Jennifer belong here.''

''You don't want her here.'' The words came out flat and accusing, and she was horrified that she'd spoken them. The last thing she needed was to set another cause of friction between them.

She waited for an explosion, but it didn't come. Oddly enough, Nathan didn't seem offended. Maybe he was one of those rare people who actually appreciated blunt honesty.

He shrugged, shoulders moving restlessly under the uniform shirt. ''I suppose I don't. Dad doesn't need to be taking care of a teenager who doesn't belong to him.''

''Doesn't belong?'' She echoed his words. What a lonely sound they had.

He frowned, looking as if he were tempted to tell her to mind her own business. But he didn't.

''Jen arrived on the bus a month ago,'' he said heavily. ''That same day a letter came from her mother, saying she was getting married again and sending Jen to stay with us while she went on her honeymoon.''

She tried to get her mind around the action. How

could a mother do that to her child? "But Jen isn't even related to you."

"Exactly. But that's her mother all over. The only thing she ever sees is what she wants."

"She doesn't sound like a very nice person." She was feeling her way, trying to understand the dynamics of the situation.

"Nice." The emphasis he put on the word made his opinion clear. "Thanks to her, the divorce practically wiped Dad out, financially and emotionally. I never understood what he saw in her. He was lonely, I guess." His voice deepened, as if he blamed himself for that.

His hand still clasped hers, as if he'd forgotten about it. She ought to pull free, but she didn't.

"I'm sorry. The situation has to be hard on all of you."

He gave a short nod. "Dad's health is already shaky. The last thing he needs is having to take care of a rebellious teenager who doesn't belong here."

She understood his feelings, but she couldn't help seeing Jen's viewpoint, too. Jen was another lost child, and lost children were Susannah's business, as well as her passion.

"It sounds as if Jennifer doesn't belong anywhere right now."

His frown deepened. "Her mother is the one who should be responsible for her."

"Her mother dumped her here." She couldn't be having this conversation with a man she barely knew. But the usual rules didn't seem to apply between them. "It's hard for you. But it's worse for her." She hesitated. "I know."

"You know," he repeated. "How do you know?"

His gaze probed, as if to look right through her. He was still holding her hand, and the pressure of his fingers seemed to repeat the question, compelling an answer.

She looked up at him. For the sake of that troubled teenager who was where she'd once been, she'd let him see the truth in her eyes.

"Because I was in Jen's place once. After my mother died, my father sent me off to boarding school, camp or anyone who would take me. Trust me, I know what it's like to be the kid no one wants."

For a moment he didn't move. Then he brushed her cheek lightly with the backs of his fingers, as if wiping away the tears she wouldn't shed. Her skin seemed to tingle where he touched.

"I'm sorry. I didn't know that happened to you, Susannah."

"I'm fine now." She struggled to swallow the lump that had formed in her throat. "But I know how Jen feels. I think that gives me the responsibility to ask you to cut her a little slack. Please. Even when she's being her most obnoxious."

His eyes stayed watchful, but his smile flickered.

"You mean like when she wants to wear black nail polish and five earrings to church?"

"That's about it."

The smile turned rueful. "I'll try. I'm not making any promises, but I'll try not to let her push my buttons so easily."

"You won't regret it, Nathan."

"I already do." He flicked a stray curl lightly with his fingertip. "You must be something in the courtroom, Ms. Morgan."

"Not bad." She could actually breathe again, now that the atmosphere had eased between them. "I work with a social services department, though. It's not as if I'm up against Clarence Darrow, for the most part."

"You're on a leave now, are you?"

"For the moment. After the baby's born, I'll have to decide when I'm going back."

And whether she'd go back. Little Sarah would have only one parent. It might be time to put her career on hold for a while.

Nathan's gaze held hers. "How about telling me something?"

She'd already told him too much. "What?"

"Why did you want to make sure I was out of sight this afternoon?"

She leaned back, putting another inch or two between them. It wasn't enough.

"You know, that's a lawyer's trick, circling back to ask a question."

"It's a cop's trick, too. I guess we actually have something in common. Now, about my question…"

He let the words hang, but his demeanor made it plain he wasn't going anywhere until she answered.

Maybe the only way to handle this was to put the truth out there between them. She smoothed the maternity sweater down over her stomach.

"Your father told me about what happened to Linda. I'm sorry." The words were inadequate. She knew that better than anyone.

"He shouldn't have." His jaw tightened.

"I know that having me here is a reminder for you. I thought it might be best if I stayed out of sight as much as I could."

He was already shaking his head before she finished. "No. Don't feel that way, please." He straightened, driving his hand through his hair, then clasping the back of his neck. "Look, I'm the one who's sorry. I confess, the first time I saw you at the cottage, it was a shock. But I'm over that now. It's fine. Really."

If she'd just been listening to his words, she might have believed that. Unfortunately, she could see the bleakness in Nathan's eyes, and she knew the truth. It wasn't fine at all.

Maybe Susannah had been right in her analysis, Nathan thought as he pulled up at the cottage Wednesday evening. Maybe this situation would be easier for him if he didn't have to see her.

They'd gotten too close in that conversation. Gotten too close, revealed too much. He didn't do that, not even with his father. Was it only Susannah's pregnancy that got under his guard?

He barely remembered the child she'd been that summer she'd come to the lake. He had a vague picture of a skinny kid with red hair and freckles—that was it.

He did remember that Linda had been good with her and Trevor when she baby-sat. But then, Linda had always been good with kids. They'd planned on having a houseful, but it hadn't worked out that way.

His fingers tightened on the steering wheel. They'd had so many disappointments, one after another. When Linda had finally become pregnant, she'd been so ecstatic that it hurt to remember.

He took a breath, forcing his fingers to relax, and left the motor running as he got out of the car. It wasn't fair to make Susannah carry the burden of thinking she was hurting him just by being here. She had enough to deal with.

So he'd take her to the covered-dish supper at church. He'd see to it she had a good time. And he'd prove to her that he wasn't bothered at all, either by her presence or her condition.

His knock at the door brought Susannah to answer it already wearing a loose jacket and carrying a box from the bakery. She looked taken aback at the sight of him.

"Nathan, hello. I thought your father was picking me up tonight."

"He and Jen went early with Rhoda to help set up for the dinner." He took the box she held. "You didn't need to bring anything. You're a visitor."

"I wanted to." She pulled the jacket around herself, smoothing her hand over her rounded figure in a gesture that had to be automatic.

Show her this doesn't bother you at all, remember? He pasted a smile on his face and took her arm to help her down the steps and into the car.

Once they'd pulled out of the lane, he glanced toward her. The sun, low in the sky, sent a pool of light across her from the side window, making that auburn hair of hers look like a flame.

"Are you hoping for a little redhead?" He forced the question out, hoping she'd get the message. He wasn't bothered at all by her pregnancy. He could talk about her baby.

"Given that she got the genes for red hair from both sides of the family, it's probably inevitable. Actually, I'd be just as happy if my little girl didn't have to put up with the teasing I did."

Her baby was a girl, then. His child, his and Linda's, had been a boy. He was in a mood to cling to differences.

"Carrottop?"

"Among others." Susannah's smile lingered, with no sharp edges to it this time. "I'm sure I'll think she's the most beautiful baby in the world, no matter what.''

She'd have her mother's beauty. The involuntary thought startled him.

At some point over the past few days he'd started noticing the curve of Susannah's cheek, the delicate modeling of her face, the quick intelligence in her eyes. Probably it would be better to go back to his initial assessment of her as a brittle yuppie who didn't belong here.

And it certainly would be better to get the conversation onto some path that didn't have him thinking about how attractive Susannah was.

''Is there anyone in particular you want to meet tonight? To talk to about Trevor, I mean.''

Her smile faded. ''Am I that obvious? I might just be going because I like church suppers.''

''You might,'' he conceded. ''But given your reason for being here, I supposed you'd take advantage of the opportunity to fill in any gaps there might be.''

Something shadowed her gaze. ''Yes, I guess so. If you know of anyone that Trevor might have talked with in those last days, I'd appreciate meeting them. I don't want to make people feel uncomfortable, though.''

He suppressed the instinct to reach across and clasp her hand. ''I think most folks understand.''

She lifted her chin and seemed to be staring at the church as he pulled into the parking lot. ''I would like to talk with the pastor. I suppose he'll be there tonight.''

''I'm sure he will.''

Good. Pastor Winstead was a professional at dealing with people in trouble. He'd know how to say all the things that Nathan couldn't seem to manage.

He got out and rounded the car, taking Susannah's arm to help her out. ''Ready for this?''

''I guess so.'' She tilted her head to smile at him. That smile seemed to hit him right in the face, and a wave of electricity strong enough to light half the town jolted through him.

Whoa. He bent to pick up the bakery box, using the moment to regain his equilibrium. He couldn't be attracted to Susannah. No way, nohow.

He straightened, closing the car door. Convince Susannah her presence didn't upset him—that was the mission for tonight. It certainly didn't include giving in to any random, totally inappropriate feelings.

''Let's go, then.'' He took her arm and led her to the double doors that opened into the social hall.

A blast of chatter reached them as they stepped inside, and he felt Susannah's hesitation through the pressure of her hand on his arm. He covered her hand with his.

''It's okay. They won't bite.''

''Right.'' Her grip tightened. ''Sorry. It's just a little intimidating, facing a whole roomful of people and not knowing a soul.''

"Well, all of them know you. Know who you are, that is."

Her eyebrows rose. "If that's meant to make me feel at ease, it doesn't."

He grinned. "Relax. You do know some people, anyway. My dad and Jen. Although I've noticed Jennifer generally pretends she doesn't know us when she's with the other kids."

"I'm sure you were the same at that age."

He opened his mouth to deny it, then realized she was probably right. "And Rhoda's here. Did you know that she worked for Trevor's family when they had the vacation house open?"

"No, I didn't." Her gaze seemed to search the crowd for the woman. "It's funny that she hasn't mentioned that to me."

He shrugged. "Not if you know Rhoda. She keeps herself to herself, as the saying goes."

Susannah seemed to be looking over his shoulder. "Here comes Jen. And she actually looks as if she intends to speak to us."

He turned. Jen was a few feet away, clearly headed for them. She wore a smile he hadn't seen on her face before, and she carried a baby.

"Hey, Susannah, look. Ms. Philips let me watch her baby for a while. Isn't he cute? You want to hold him?" She thrust the child toward Susannah.

"He's adorable!" Susannah's arms curved around the baby, and she turned toward him as if wanting to share the pleasure. "Isn't he?"

His whole body tensed, and he fought to look at ease.

"Sure is." He tried to smile. "Maybe you ought to take him back to his mother now."

Jen frowned at his suggestion, then carefully took the baby back, bouncing the child in her arms. "Not yet. I'm going to show Daniel."

She turned away, and he could breathe again. Could congratulate himself that no one had seen that betraying reaction.

Then he met Susannah's gaze and realized he couldn't congratulate himself after all. Susannah had seen, and she was watching him with something that looked remarkably like pity written across her face.

Chapter Five

Nathan's instinctive reaction to the infant hit Susannah right in the heart. He was struggling to smile, trying to cover it up, but she'd seen. She knew.

She reached toward him, hand out in comfort, and then drew back. Comforting Nathan right now was an impossible task, at least for her. His grief was beyond anything her sympathy would mend.

"Nathan…" She had to say something.

"Here's Dad." He turned away. "Excuse me. I see someone I need to talk with." He was gone in an instant, as if he fled from whatever pity he saw in her face.

Daniel's footsteps had been silent on the beige carpet, masked by the chatter of people and the clatter of dishes. He touched her arm. "Everything okay?"

"I guess so." She tried to pull herself together.

"He always does that." Daniel looked after his son, who was weaving purposefully through the crowd away from them. Susannah suspected Nathan didn't have a destination in mind. Just away.

"You saw what happened, then."

He nodded.

"It's as if his future died with that baby." Tears glistened in Daniel's eyes, and he wiped them away with a hand that shook slightly. "Sorry. Seems like I get a little too emotional lately."

Since his heart attack. That would bring emotions to the surface in anyone. But Daniel's face had tightened and paled enough to concern her, and she wanted to do something to ease his pain.

She patted his arm. "He's your son. Of course you get emotional when you see his grief. But you can't carry that burden for him."

"It's not just that." He met her eyes, and she realized there was guilt on his face. "I made things worse. I gambled away the only thing he had left to hold on to after he lost Linda and the baby."

For a moment she was so startled she couldn't speak. "Daniel—"

"Oh, I don't mean I've been running off to Atlantic City to hit the casinos. Nathan might actually understand that. What I did was marry a woman who didn't care two pins for the life we had here." His mouth tightened in a way that made him look very like his son. "We used to own the whole mountain.

After the divorce, we were lucky to hold on to the lodge itself.''

Her mind was whirling with the implications of that. No wonder Nathan had trouble warming up to his stepsister, with that trouble between them.

''I'm sure Nathan doesn't blame you.''

He shrugged. ''Not in so many words. But he loved that land from the time he was just a boy. He and Linda had plans to expand the lodge, put in a nature preserve, do all kinds of things with it. I lost all that with my foolishness, and the land was his last tie to his and Linda's dream.''

She didn't know what to say. ''I'm sorry.''

It was his turn to pat her arm. ''No, I'm the one who's sorry. I shouldn't have unloaded all that on you, I guess. I just wanted you to see that Nathan has reasons for acting the way he does sometimes.''

The clink of spoon on glass put a halt to anything she might have said in response. And she wasn't sure what that would have been, in any case.

Pastor Winstead waved the crowd to silence, welcomed everyone and began the blessing. Susannah tried to concentrate on the prayer, instead of letting her mind dwell on what Daniel had told her or wander to how she could strike up a conversation with the pastor and whether he'd talk to her about Trevor.

A clatter of dishes announced that the meal had begun. It was Daniel who steered her to the long, plastic-covered serving table, Daniel who introduced her to anyone who might have known Trevor. Nathan managed to put himself at the back of the line, well away from her.

Well, fine. She didn't want him to feel responsibility for her, in any event. She could handle this herself.

People worked their way down both sides of the table, filled to the groaning point with dishes. Traditional baked corn pudding steamed gently next to a platter full of nachos and a glass bowl of Greek salad—something for everyone, obviously. Susannah tried to pick and choose carefully, but even so her plate was full before she'd reached the midpoint.

She glanced up from a casserole of beans and franks to realize that Rhoda was across from her, helping a preteen boy to a hot dog. The boy looked up, giving her the generous smile that was so typical of a Down's syndrome child.

"Hi."

"Hi, yourself. My name is Susannah. What's your name?"

Rhoda put a protective arm around the boy. "This is Thomas. My son." She turned him away, putting the plate carefully in his hands. "You go sit down. Mommy will be there in a minute."

It was almost as if Rhoda wanted to protect the boy from her. Maybe she'd been subjected to too many insensitive remarks to take kindly to strangers talking to her son.

The silence stretched awkwardly, and Susannah searched for something else to say.

"Nathan told me that you used to work for Trevor's family when they summered at the lake. I'm afraid I didn't remember you from the summer I was here."

"No reason you should." Rhoda averted her eyes, and her tone was almost short enough to be rude.

She tried again. "I suppose you talked with Trevor when he was here in the spring."

Rhoda shrugged. "A bit."

"I wondered—"

She stopped. There wasn't any point in going on, when Rhoda clearly considered the conversation over. She had picked up her plate and headed for the table to join her son without a backward glance.

Well. Possibly Rhoda just didn't like strangers. But the woman's attitude seemed odd, to say the least.

She reached the end of the line, then followed Daniel to a table. He pulled out a chair for her.

"You sit here, and we'll save this one for Nathan. No need to keep a seat for Jen. She'll want to eat with the other kids."

She suspected Nathan might find a reason to sit elsewhere, too, but before she'd been introduced to everyone at the table, he'd set his plate down next to hers.

"Did you find everything you wanted?" he asked.

She nodded. "It looks wonderful."

She gestured to her plate, determined to keep the

tone light and impersonal. She and Nathan had intruded on each other's personal space too often lately.

He nodded. "Good thing I don't eat this way every day, or I wouldn't be able to reach the table." He seemed equally determined to sound natural.

She almost replied that she already couldn't reach the table, but censored herself. Still, ignoring her pregnancy was hardly a solution. Nathan had surely figured out a coping mechanism to deal with that.

Or not. She seemed to feel again his instinctive recoil when Jen had brought the baby to them. Maybe he wasn't coping as well as he'd like to believe.

Nathan was talking with someone across the table, giving her a chance to take a covert glance at him. His face was outwardly relaxed, and his right hand gestured easily with his fork.

But from this angle she could see the tension in his jaw and the way his left hand clenched against his leg. It was as if he had to armor himself against her.

No. Nathan wasn't coping at all. He'd stored his pain away in the hope that no one could see it, until her presence had brought it out of hiding. He was making a valiant effort to suppress it again, but not quite succeeding.

It's as if his future died. Daniel's words resounded in her mind.

If your future died, then you were stuck in that

painful past. A wave of something close to terror went through her. If she didn't find out the truth...

Please.

She didn't realize she was praying until the words formed in her mind.

Please let me find out what was going on with Trevor. I have to know in order to move on. I have to. If I don't, I'll be frozen where I am, just like Nathan is.

By the time the supper ended, discouragement was setting in. Although Susannah had met plenty of nice, helpful people, none of them seemed to have spent much time with Trevor on his visits, or to have anything useful to contribute.

She'd hoped to speak further with Rhoda in this relaxed setting. But Rhoda had continued to be elusive. Each time Susannah got near her, Rhoda managed to find something she must do that sent her in the opposite direction.

At least, as people began filtering out the door, Pastor Winstead became more accessible. She worked her way toward him, rehearsing in her mind ways to bring up the subject of Trevor's appointment with him.

"Mrs. Laine." The pastor slid off the folding table he'd been sitting on and held out his hand, a smile creasing his face.

"Susannah, please."

"Susannah, I'm glad you decided to join us to-night. I'll bet Daniel talked you into it, didn't he?"

"He's pretty persuasive."

The pastor seemed even younger in jeans and a sweater than he had standing behind the pulpit in his robe on Sunday morning. With his easy grin and tousled sandy hair, he looked more like a college student than a minister.

She began to have doubts. Would Trevor really have confided in him?

"I'm so sorry about your loss. Trevor will certainly be missed."

He clasped her hand warmly in both of his as he spoke. A wave of sympathy seemed to envelop her.

Susannah revised her opinion. Eric Winstead might be young, but he projected a presence and an empathy that belied his years.

"Thank you." For an instant her throat tightened in grief. "You knew Trevor, then."

He nodded. "We met on the two occasions he was here in the spring. I can certainly understand why you felt you needed to come to Lakemont. I hope it's providing some solace to you."

"Everyone has been very kind. I've appreciated being able to talk to people who saw Trevor when he was in Lakemont." She still didn't have a persuasive way of asking what she needed to. Maybe she'd just better open the subject and see how he responded. "I know that Trevor intended to make an appointment to talk with you."

Eric Winstead's gaze seemed to probe her face, as if seeking some answers of his own. "Yes, he did make an appointment."

A silent prayer filled her mind. *Please. Let him be honest with me.*

"I realize you may not want to discuss it, but I hope you'll tell me what the two of you talked about."

Holding her breath, she waited for a response.

For a long moment the minister seemed to weigh her words in some balance, frowning slightly. Then he shook his head, and her heart sank.

"Trevor did make an appointment to come and talk with me." Sorrow etched his face. "But he died the night before we were going to meet. I'm so sorry."

Disappointment gripped her heart. Trevor might have confided in this man, but he hadn't had the chance. And she was beginning to fear that whatever secrets Trevor had been hiding, they had died with him.

"Susannah?"

The sound of Nathan's voice cut through her pain. She turned, to realize he was standing right behind her. Her pulse accelerated. How much had he overheard?

She pasted a smile on her face. "Have you been waiting for me?"

"No hurry." He glanced from her to the pastor. "I can wait, if the two of you aren't finished."

"No, I'm ready to leave if you are." She extended her hand to Pastor Winstead. "Thank you. I'm glad we had an opportunity to talk."

"Come in anytime." He held her hand a moment longer, as if in wordless apology for not being able to help. "I'd be happy to see you."

She nodded, turning away, trying to put a cheerful facade on her discouragement. She had the ride home to get through, and she certainly didn't want to raise any questions in Nathan's mind.

Nathan held her jacket for her, and she slipped it on. For just an instant his hands rested on her shoulders. She heard the soft inhale of his breath, sensed that he was about to ask her something.

She took a quick step away. "Okay, I'm ready. Is anyone else riding back with us?"

If he knew she was evading him, he didn't show it. "No, Rhoda drove Jen and Dad home. It's just the two of us."

She nodded, then moved toward the door. Just the two of them. If Nathan had overheard her questioning the minister, he'd have plenty of time to bring it up.

Outside, the streetlights cast pools of pale yellow on the nearly deserted parking lot. Now that the sun had gone down, the air had turned chilly. Their footsteps echoed on the concrete.

Nathan reached past her to open the car door, his arm brushing hers. He held the door for her in frowning silence, then went around and got behind the wheel, still without speaking.

She took a deep breath, feeling her tension ease as Nathan turned onto the road for the short drive along the lake to the lodge. They passed the turnoff to the ruins of the old Laine house. He glanced at her. She could see the movement of his head, but not his expression in the dark.

"Have you and Enid decided what you're going to do about the property here?"

"Not yet."

Actually, she hadn't even talked to Enid about it. She hadn't wanted to raise any questions about Lakemont in Enid's mind. His silence seemed to be pressing for more of an answer than that.

"I have a feeling she won't want to sell. Enid doesn't like—well, changes, I guess. She seems to want to keep things the way her late husband had them."

"Did Trevor agree with that?"

What was Nathan getting at? Tension trickled along her nerves.

"He did most of the time, I suppose. He always felt that his mother had to be protected from anything unpleasant. If she didn't want to sell the property, he wouldn't have pushed the idea."

"But he came to look at the place. He must have had something in mind."

It was the first time he'd come even close to asking why Trevor had been here, and she struggled to find a response that would head off that line of thought.

"Trevor was a very responsible person," she said carefully. "He'd want to look into the situation thoroughly before he suggested any course of action."

"Responsibility is an admirable quality."

"Yes, it is." Did he think that a lukewarm description, coming from a widow about her husband?

The car nosed into the lane that swept past the lodge toward the cottage, and she felt like pushing the vehicle forward. Anything to get this drive over with. She wanted to be alone to decide what she should do next. She certainly didn't want to fence with Nathan.

"Well, thanks so much for driving me to the covered dish. I enjoyed it." She buttoned her jacket, ready to escape the minute they reached the cottage.

Nathan stopped the car and turned off the ignition. By the time she'd unbuckled her seat belt, he'd come around to open the door for her. He took her arm to help her out.

"I'm not made of glass, you know." Irritation touched her voice. "I can still get out of a car on my own."

Gravel slid under her feet as she tried to stand, and the fact that she had to struggle to keep her balance undercut her words.

"I'm sure you can." His expression was hidden from her in the darkness, but she wasn't sure she liked the steely note in his voice. "I thought you might invite me in."

Short of being outright rude, she couldn't do anything but nod. They moved into the pool of light cast by the porch lamp she'd left on, and she could see his face.

Reluctance. Determination. He really didn't want to enter the cottage at all. But he would, because something was driving him.

Susannah walked quickly inside, slipping out of her jacket and dropping it on the nearest chair. She switched on the table lamp, and the cozy room sprang to welcoming life around them. Darkness pressed against the sliding glass doors in absolute contrast.

Then her perspective seemed to change, and she saw the glass panels as mirrors, reflecting the warm room and their two figures standing a few feet apart. Nathan was frowning, arms folded, looking as immovable as a rock.

With a quick movement she crossed to the doors and pulled the drapery cord. The swish of off-white vertical blinds shut out both the darkness outside and the reflected scene.

"Would you like some coffee?" She managed a hostesslike smile as she turned toward Nathan. "It will only take a few minutes to make some."

"No. I don't want coffee." He took a step toward her, his expression firm. "And I don't want to chat. I want to know what you're doing here."

Her heart began to thud against her ribs. "I don't know what you mean."

He shook his head impatiently, another long stride bringing him close enough that she could feel the air of command surrounding him, demanding answers.

"That won't do, Susannah." His implacable expression told her he wouldn't be satisfied with less than the truth. "You let all of us believe you were here as part of mourning your husband's death. You're not. You're conducting an investigation. And I want to know why."

Chapter Six

Nathan watched Susannah's expressive face react to his challenge. Shock, then something that might have been fear. And then determination.

"I don't know what you're talking about." She turned away from him, crossing her arms.

"Yes, you do." He suppressed the urge to take her arm and turn her back to face him. Touching her would be a bad move, for more reasons than he cared to assess. "You know exactly what I'm talking about. You're trying to find out something about Trevor's visit here."

She swung toward him, lifting her chin. Her heart-shaped face was pale and stern. "Even if that were true, it's certainly none of your business."

"You made it my business when you started using my family."

He saw that arrow strike home. Susannah's lashes swept down to hide her eyes, her defiance faltering.

"No. I'm not—I didn't intend to use anyone."

"But you did." He pressed the advantage. "You questioned my father. You used us as an entrée to people in our church family. You even questioned the pastor."

"I think Pastor Winstead is well able to take care of himself." The words were tart, but her fingers twisted together.

"That's not the point, and you know it. What's going on, Susannah?"

He felt the strength of her will holding out against him. If Susannah continued to stonewall, he couldn't force her to speak.

Suddenly she shook her head. The lines deepened in her face, as if she were too exhausted to keep resisting him.

"I had to come." She clenched her hands in front of her, her eyes darkening with passion. "I had to know why Trevor was here."

"But—" For a moment he didn't follow. "You mean you don't know why he came?"

Anger flashed in her eyes, and he didn't know if it was for herself or him or Trevor. "I mean I didn't know he was here at all. He didn't tell me he was coming to Lakemont. He lied to me."

The anger and defiance seemed to go out of her all at once, and her whole body sagged. Alarmed, he caught her arm and lowered her to the sofa, sitting down next to her. She seemed very fragile suddenly.

"I'm sorry." The words seemed inadequate, but he didn't know what else to say. His mind revolved around her revelation.

Well, there was an obvious reason most men lied about something like this.

"I know what you're thinking." She straightened, pulling her shoulders back. "What anyone would think. But it's not true. Trevor wouldn't do that."

"I'm sure there's an innocent explanation." Although he couldn't seem to think of one.

"Don't patronize me!" She swung toward him, her bronze hair flying out as if in exclamation as anger sparked in her eyes again.

"I'm not." But he was, wasn't he?

"That's part of the reason I didn't want anyone to know the truth. Because you'd just pat me on the head and assure me everything was fine, all the while believing Trevor was having an affair."

"All right." She had a point. That was probably exactly what he'd have done. "I won't patronize you. Let's just stick to the facts." He tried a smile. "An attorney and a cop ought to be pretty good at that, don't you think?"

She didn't smile back, but he could sense some of the tension seep out of her. Susannah could tell him it was none of his business, but she didn't. Instead she nodded, clasping her hands in front of her like a little girl who was about to recite.

"Facts. As far as I've been able to find out, Trevor made two visits to Lakemont in the spring, staying at Sloane Lodge both times. The first time he was here only two days, the second for nearly a week."

That was why she'd wanted access to the lodge register, obviously.

"Those are the only times he's been at the lodge." He'd have certainly known if Trevor had been there on any other occasion. He couldn't have missed that.

"I didn't know he was here either time." She said the words as if they tasted bitter on her tongue.

"Where did you think he was?" He carefully kept anything resembling sympathy from his tone.

"The first visit was apparently added on to a business trip Trevor made to Pittsburgh. The second time he told me he was going to a business conference in Boston. He didn't. He came here." She looked at him then, and he read clearly the grief and pain that darkened her eyes. "He lied to me. I have to know why he lied to me."

"I'm sorry," he said again. What a mess this was. He touched her shoulder lightly, wanting to comfort her and not knowing how.

She moved convulsively, then put her hand over her mouth as if to hold back a sob.

"It's okay," he said softly. "Anybody would cry over that. You don't have to be strong on my account."

She shook her head, wiping tears away with her fingers. "I have to be strong for myself. And for the baby." She looked at him then, her face open and vulnerable. "Don't you see? I can't go on with my life unless I know the truth, no matter what it is."

"Susannah..."

He didn't want to say anything. In fact, what he wanted to do was get up and walk out. Run out, even. He couldn't help her.

But he'd forced her confidence, and she'd opened up to him. She might be the last woman in the world he'd ever expect to get close to, but it was too late for that. It had already happened.

He touched her shoulder lightly, feeling the tension that had her tied in knots. "You have to face the fact that you might never find out."

It might be better for her if she could give up on this quest. Maybe better for everyone.

"I have to know." Her lips firmed. "I'm not leaving until I know why Trevor lied to me. I can deal with anything, as long as I know the truth."

She had a lot more courage than most people would in her situation. Most people, he thought, would prefer never to find out for sure, so that they could believe the comforting stories they told themselves.

"I think you can."

Susannah fixed her gaze on his face, and he couldn't possibly look away. "In that case, will you help me?"

He should say no. He should get up from the sofa, walk out the door and never look back. His every instinct told him that nothing good could come from this.

But he couldn't. As sure as he was that he was going to regret it and that she was going to get hurt, he couldn't say no.

"All right." He hoped he didn't sound as reluctant as he felt. "If that's what it takes to bring this to an end for you. I'll help you."

It had been difficult enough to say he'd help Susannah. Actually doing so might be downright impossible. Nathan sat in his office the next afternoon, staring out the window at Main Street.

A cluster of teenage boys went by, roughhousing with each other, probably in relief that school was out for the day. An older couple, jostled by their behavior, had to step aside to make room for them, and he frowned, making a mental note of the boys' identities.

He'd have said, if pressed, that he knew most of the people in Lakemont, knew much of what went on in his town. Those boys, for instance.

The ringleader was one of the Ferguson kids, and each of his three older brothers had had some slight brush with the law. It looked as if Thad leaned toward following the family tradition.

Yes, he knew his people, all right—knew who was likely to be involved in petty theft or vandalism, knew whose alcoholism endangered his marriage, knew who had visitors when her husband was out of town.

But tracking down the movements of a casual visitor six months ago was something else again. Susannah seemed to have confidence in his ability to help her. He wasn't so sure about that, and he definitely wasn't convinced that her mission was a good idea.

Her face rose in his mind, green eyes flashing with determination. Susannah was a fighter who wouldn't give up.

Footsteps crossed the outer office, and the tall figure of his assistant chief appeared in the doorway. "You working in here, or just brooding?"

He shoved himself back from the desk and stood. He trusted Jared Stark as much as anyone in his life. And Jared might have some ideas about what Trevor Laine had done in Lakemont.

"Maybe a little of both." He rounded the desk and leaned against it. "You remember Trevor Laine?"

Jared nodded, eyes narrowing in concentration.

That made it easier, but still Nathan chose his words carefully. Susannah's secret wasn't his to tell.

"I need to find out what he did when he was in Lakemont before he died. Any ideas?"

Jared frowned. "You care to tell me why?"

"I'm trying to help his wife." He didn't have to say more, not to Jared.

"Okay." The frown lingered. "I remember seeing him a couple of times, around town. I talked to him once. He acted like he remembered me, but I didn't think he knew who I was, not really."

"What made you think that?"

Jared shrugged. "He was coming out of the café when I spoke to him. He just looked at me for a minute, like what I said didn't even register. Seemed like he was a man with something on his mind."

A man with something on his mind. One who'd made an appointment to talk with the minister. One who'd lied to his wife about where he was going. It didn't look promising for finding an innocent explanation.

"You know, I saw him at the café a couple of times, now that I think about it." Jared lifted his brows. "Maybe you ought to talk to Evelyn."

They both knew that Evelyn Standish, owner of the Cozy Corner Café, made it her business to know something about everyone who crossed her path.

"Guess I should try that." He rubbed the back of his neck, where tension seemed to have taken up residence. "Not that I think I'll actually find out anything. No reason anyone should have noticed what a casual visitor was doing, or remember it if they did notice."

"It's important to Mrs. Laine, is it?" Jared seemed to be reading between the lines of what he didn't say, but Jared was safe.

He nodded. "It's important. I just wish I knew what to say to her."

He needed some magic words that would ease his conscience and send Susannah away at peace with Trevor's death. There was small chance of finding words that would do that.

"It looks to me as if you'd better think of something fast." Jared was staring past him, through the window. "Because if this pregnant lady coming down the street's Mrs. Laine, it sure looks like she's headed here."

A quick glance told him Jared had it right. Susannah was headed straight for the police station, and she didn't look as if anything, including the rambunctious teenagers who still loitered on the walk, would deter her.

With her chin tilted and her hair touched bronze by the sun, she reminded him of Joan of Arc marching into battle. Even the betraying roundness of her pregnancy didn't mar the picture of determination.

Jared was right. He'd better think of something.

By the time he reached the front office, Susannah was already coming in the door. Her gaze glanced off Jared and came to rest on him.

"I hope you don't mind my stopping by. I thought you might have time to talk."

No convenient excuse popped to mind. "Of course." He gestured. "This is Jared Stark, my assistant chief. Jared, Susannah Laine."

They shook hands, and he noted the quick way

Jared assessed her. It would be interesting to hear Jared's reactions to Susannah. His own reactions were too clouded with mixed emotions to be relied upon.

Jared was already headed for the door. "I'll just take a quick walk around downtown, Chief."

Nathan nodded, then turned back to Susannah. "Come into my office."

He ushered her in and followed her, pausing in the doorway to try to see the room through her eyes. It was broom-closet-sized, with a dented gray metal desk that looked like army surplus and probably was. He had a bulletin board cluttered with too many notices. The computer was the only thing up-to-date.

He closed the door, giving them a small amount of privacy in case anyone came into the station. "I guess this is not the sort of office you're used to."

She looked at him, brows rising. "I work for a social services agency, remember? There's never enough funding, and I share a cubbyhole with two social workers. Believe me, we can't even all stretch at the same time."

He held his battered wooden visitor's chair for her. "You do know what it's like, then, living on a government budget. Here I was picturing you in some fancy office with mahogany furniture and Oriental carpets."

Her smile flickered. "That doesn't happen in my line of work."

"It could, couldn't it?" His curiosity slipped off

its leash. "I mean, you could be working for a big law firm in the city."

"I could, if I wanted to spend twelve hours a day helping people with too much money and too little sense trying to untangle their messes." She looked challengingly at him. "Or are you thinking those are my kind of people?"

He leaned against his desk and held up his hands in a gesture of surrender. "Just curious, that's all. When I first saw you—"

He stopped. Maybe he shouldn't go there.

"When you first saw me, you thought I was a spoiled rich woman come to clutter up your time schedule for closing the lodge."

"Well, maybe something like that."

Her smile faded a little. "I haven't forgotten the promise I made you. If you're ready to close the lodge after this coming weekend, I'll check out. I can probably find a room in town."

That was what he wanted, wasn't it? Somehow he wasn't so sure any longer. His need to protect his father battled with the obligation he felt to help Susannah. But Dad continued to resist his efforts, while Susannah—

He shook his head. Maybe he already knew the answer to this one.

"You don't need to do that. If we haven't come up with any answers by then—well, maybe it's still better to stay where you are."

Those green eyes of hers assessed him. "Because you want to keep an eye on me?"

Maybe that was partly true, but he didn't intend to admit it to her.

"Because there's no point in making a move for a matter of a couple of weeks. If we haven't found out what you need to know by then…"

He left it open, because he really didn't know the ending to that.

"I'll have to leave." A shadow crossed her face. "My doctor doesn't want me to travel any closer to my due date. And if I go back, not knowing…" She paused, her somber look intensifying. "Then I suppose I never will know."

He'd thought he wanted her to leave at any cost. But maybe that cost was too high.

If she'd been the woman he'd first thought she was, that might have been okay.

She wasn't. She was determined—he certainly knew that about her. Given the work she'd chosen to do, she must have a crusading streak a mile wide.

And he'd begun to see that, in spite of the secrets she'd withheld from him, she was a fundamentally honest person who needed to know the truth.

"I hope we can find out." He spoke carefully, wanting to encourage her without giving false hope. "But it's possible no one noticed what Trevor did here."

"I have to try."

"I know." He planted his hands behind him on

the edge of the desk. "I talked to Jared about it, just in a general way. I didn't tell him why I was asking."

"Did he know anything?"

"He remembered seeing Trevor in the café a couple of times. Evelyn, the owner, is the kind of person who always wants to know everyone's business."

She stood almost before he had the words out. "Then let's go talk to her."

"Maybe you'd better let me handle this."

"Why?" She fired the question at him.

There was no good way to say this. "People might talk more easily to me if you're not there."

He pushed away from the desk, the movement bringing him close to her. Too close. He could smell the light flowery scent that clung to her skin, see the small lines form between her brows.

"Because they might think…"

She looked up at him, then seemed to lose track of whatever she'd intended to say. Her eyes darkened.

He reached toward her, his hand moving before the thought formed. She seemed to sway toward him. In a moment she'd be in his arms.

The outer door slammed. "Nathan? Are you here?"

Jen's voice was like a splash of cold water in his face. He took a clumsy step backward, bumping into the desk.

This looked as if it would be the first time he'd ever been happy to see his stepsister. Because if she hadn't barged in, he might have done something he'd be a long time regretting.

Chapter Seven

Susannah grasped the back of the wooden chair for support as Jen surged into the office. She turned away, needing to hide her expression from both Nathan and Jen for a few precious seconds, at least.

But turning away didn't help. Now she faced the wide window of Nathan's office that looked out onto the street. Had she really been about to fall into Nathan's arms in full view of anyone walking down Main Street?

What on earth was wrong with her? She'd been a widow only six months, and she was expecting Trevor's child. She couldn't possibly be attracted to another man, even one as appealing as Nathan. And particularly not with the shadow of Trevor's deceit hanging over her head.

Focus, she commanded herself. She couldn't begin to explain these erratic emotions, and she certainly couldn't guess at what Nathan's reactions to her were. Maybe all of this was on her side.

She felt her cheeks warm at the thought. Her only possible option was to ignore the whole subject and hope Nathan would do the same.

Composing her face, she turned slowly to face Nathan and Jen, only to discover that neither of them had the slightest interest in her actions. The tiny office was crowded with the three of them in it, but they were too engrossed in their quarrel with each other to pay attention to her.

"You don't have to make a federal case out of it just 'cause the bus left without me." Jen flung out her arms with a gesture worthy of a drama class.

"The bus didn't leave without you." Nathan's jaw looked almost too tight for speech. "You deliberately missed the bus. What were you doing?"

"Nothing." Jen's face turned sulky. "Just talking to some kids, that's all."

"What kids?"

"It's none of your business who I talk to," Jen flared back, taking instant offense.

It was really too bad that neither of them could view the quarrel from her point of view. She couldn't help but see that Nathan and Jen brought out the worst in each other. They both came into every encounter so ready to fight that a rational conversation was impossible.

Had she been that way with her father after her mother's death? Maybe, although her father had been so detached it had been almost impossible to argue with him, no matter how she'd tried. And of course she'd tried, longing for any attention from him, even if it was negative.

Maybe the right word for him had been defeated, not detached. He simply hadn't been able to care.

That wasn't the situation with Nathan. He cared, even though he didn't want to, or Jen's actions wouldn't bother him so much. But she didn't think he would admit that caring. Maybe he didn't even recognize it himself.

As for Jen—Susannah knew only too well what Jen was feeling. Lost. Adrift.

"Look." She interrupted the quarrel that had gone far beyond the subject of Jen's missing the bus.

They turned to her, seeming startled at the reminder that she was still in the room.

"It seems to me the immediate problem is to get Jen back to the lodge. I'm going there now, so I can take her."

Jen looked mulishly determined to continue the battle with Nathan, but he sent Susannah a harassed look accompanied by a quick nod.

"Thanks. I'd take her, but I can't leave the office until Jared gets back." He swung back to Jen. "Go home with Susannah. We'll talk later."

Jen opened her mouth, then apparently thought better of whatever she'd been about to say. Instead, she whirled and flounced out of the office. In an instant they heard the outer door slam.

The telephone rang a minute later, and Nathan turned to pick it up, holding up his hand to her in an indication that she should wait. "Chief Sloane."

An agitated murmur came across the line, barely reaching her ears, and Nathan frowned.

"No, Dad, it's all right. Don't get upset. Jen's here, and Susannah's going to drive her home."

He listened for another moment, concern darkening his eyes. "It doesn't do any good for you to make yourself sick over it. Just relax. She'll be home soon."

Susannah's heart sank. Clearly Daniel had been upset over Jen's failure to appear on the bus. Just as clearly, that wouldn't help Nathan's relationship with Jen.

"I'm sorry," she said as he hung up. "Your father was worried."

"Yes." His scowl would certainly be enough to make her think twice about anything she'd been doing. "This business with Jen can't go on."

"Nathan—"

"Sorry. It's not your concern."

He was right. It wasn't. And yet she couldn't stop longing to help them.

Nathan touched her hand lightly, his expression softening. "About the other—I'll talk with Evelyn as soon as I get a chance."

If he remembered what had happened when they'd talked about that earlier, he obviously didn't intend to let it show. Or maybe he hadn't felt a thing.

"Fine." She managed a smile. "Thanks." Afraid her own face might be showing too much, she turned and hurried after Jen.

The girl's quick movement had taken her right out of the police station, but now she stood on the walk, her dramatic exit ruined by not knowing where Susannah's car was.

Probably the best thing Susannah could do was treat the whole thing casually. "My car is parked down this way," she said, nodding down the street.

Jen fell into step, her black boots clacking defiantly on the sidewalk. After half a block in silence, the girl shot a sideways glance at her.

"Is your baby due pretty soon?"

"In about five weeks." Remembering the way the girl's face had lit up over the baby at the church supper, she realized this might be a way past Jen's guard. "It feels like forever. I wish I could hold her in my arms right now."

"A little girl? What are you going to call her?"

"Sarah Grace." She smiled, touching her side where the baby was kicking. "Sarah for my mother, and Grace—well, just because I hope she'll be filled with grace."

"That's nice." Jen stared down at her deep purple nails. "I don't think I was named for any special reason."

She shouldn't judge the girl's mother without

meeting her, but she couldn't help feeling that Jen had been shortchanged in the parenting department. They'd reached the car, so she waited until they'd gotten in and she'd pulled onto Main Street toward the lodge before she tried to respond.

"You know, some people just pick a baby's name because they like the way it sounds," she said casually. "Jennifer is a pretty name."

"It's wimpy." Jen's voice was filled with disdain. "That's why I told all the kids here to call me Jen."

"I guess you're getting to know some kids at school now." She said the words cautiously, mindful of the girl's reaction to Nathan's questions about her friends. Still, she could understand Nathan's concern.

"Yeah." Jen brooded for a moment. "It's hard, you know?" She glanced across at Susannah, and Susannah caught the vulnerability in her eyes. "Everybody here already has their own special friends— people they've known for about a million years."

Susannah remembered only too well trying to break into the crowd, any crowd, at the boarding school where she'd been sent. Nobody had seemed to have time for a grieving newcomer with a sulky attitude, especially one who didn't want to be there.

"I know. It's like they're speaking a language they understand and you don't."

"It is like that. I met this guy, the one I was talking to after school. Thad. He seemed pretty cool, but then he went off with some other kids like I wasn't even there.''

Jennifer blinked rapidly, as if there were tears in her eyes that she didn't intend to shed.

''It's really tough to break in.'' If Jen would only show this vulnerability to Nathan, he might be more sympathetic. Or not. She just wasn't sure.

''I can't get to know anybody if I have to go straight back to the lodge after school every day.'' Jennifer's resentment flared.

''What about working on the youth group float? Seems as if that would be a good way to get acquainted.''

Jen shrugged. ''Can't be there unless I have a ride, can I?''

''Why don't I take you?'' That would be a small enough return for everything Nathan and his father had been doing for her.

Jen's head came up, her gaze suspicious. ''What's in it for you?''

Susannah's heart clenched. *Lord, this child can't even accept a simple gift without looking for strings.*

''I'm not busy. I don't need anything in return.''

''Most people do.''

''Not all. Not Daniel.'' She held her breath, wondering if she should say anything about Daniel's call. But she'd probably already gone too far into their tangled relationships.

Jen brooded on that for a moment, as if she found Daniel's actions incomprehensible. ''Well, Daniel's different from most people. If you're going to drive me around, I should do something for you.''

That was a good sign, wasn't it, that Jen wanted to return a favor? She scoured her brain for something she could let the girl do in return.

''Tell you what. If you really want to do something for me, you can keep me company when I have to go for a doctor's appointment. My doctor back home made me promise I'd see someone here.'' She made a face. ''I hate going to someone new.''

Jen seemed to look at the offer from all angles. ''Okay,'' she said finally. ''You've got a deal.'' She smiled suddenly, the look wiping away all the pseudosophistication and giving a glimpse of the girl she was beneath.

Susannah's heart clenched again. If only Nathan could see that smile.

But he never would, because he was just as guarded as Jennifer was. Or more. Both of them kept a barricade around their feelings, probably for the same reason—to keep from getting hurt.

Perhaps she had begun to breach Jen's shell. Unfortunately, she couldn't expect to do the same with Nathan. He was too well armored ever to let her get that close.

Nathan walked across the parking lot toward the lodge a couple of hours after Jen and Susannah left his office. He could only be grateful that he'd had

time to regain his equilibrium before encountering
Susannah again.

How had he let himself get that close to the
woman? If they hadn't been interrupted, he'd have
been holding her in his arms in full view of Main
Street. That would really have set the gossips talking.

Not that where it had happened really made it any
worse. The fact that it had happened was already
bad enough. He didn't intend to become involved
with anyone again, and even if he did, it certainly
wouldn't be with a woman who was pregnant with
another man's child.

All right. He knew where he stood. All he had to
do was keep a choke collar on his reactions when
Susannah was around. And spending as little time
as possible with her would certainly help that along.

He stepped into the front hall. Susannah sat on
the deacon's bench against the wall, a newspaper on
her lap. She wasn't reading. She was waiting for
him.

She stood as he approached, smoothing the soft
fabric of the rust-colored jumper she wore. "Nathan.
Do you have a minute?"

He would absolutely not notice the creamy texture
of her skin, or imagine how it would feel to cup her
cheek with his hand.

Concentrate. Susannah probably expected him to
have answers already from Evelyn.

"I'm sorry I haven't had a chance to speak to

Evelyn yet.'' He took a swift glance around the hallway, but no one else was there. ''By the time I could have gone to the café, she'd have been getting busy with the evening meal. I figured that wasn't a good time to try for her undivided attention.''

''No, I didn't expect you'd have had a chance to talk with her yet. I thought of something else.''

He had a sinking feeling that whatever it was, he wasn't going to like it. ''What?''

''Where was Trevor going on the evening he died?'' She asked the question as if it were important.

''I don't know.'' He frowned, wondering what she was getting at. ''He could have been going anywhere. He was only a couple of miles from town.''

She shook her head, clearly impatient with him. ''I don't know why this didn't occur to me before. Maybe it's that famous pregnancy fuzzy thinking.''

''I don't see why you feel it's so important.''

She was grasping at straws, but he didn't want to tell her that.

''Look, I'd been making an assumption that Trevor was leaving for Philadelphia when he had the accident.''

''Right. He was headed in that direction, anyway.''

''But the pastor said he had an appointment with Trevor for the next day, so Trevor couldn't have been leaving.'' She leaned toward him. ''Don't you see that?''

He saw, all right, and his heart sank. None of the possibilities that occurred to him were ones he wanted to share with her.

"I don't know. That road leads to the county seat, then picks up the interstate. It made sense to assume he was headed home. His bags were in the car."

Susannah rubbed her arms, as if chilled. "He'd called earlier that day. I thought from Boston. He'd said to expect him in a couple of days."

A couple of days Trevor had planned to spend somewhere he didn't want to tell his wife about.

Susannah frowned, her gaze locking on his face. "You think he was going somewhere with a woman."

"I didn't say that." He was only too aware of how weak his protest sounded. "Look, there could be a dozen explanations. You may never know where he was headed."

Her mouth tightened with resolve. "I have to." She turned suddenly, picking up the handbag that lay on the bench behind her.

"Where are you going?" He suspected he wouldn't like the answer.

"I want to see the accident site for myself."

She started to move around him, and he caught her arm.

Don't touch, remember? Stay away from her.

Sound advice. Unfortunately he couldn't take it. "That's not a good idea."

Her face set stubbornly. "I'm going."

He didn't want to do this. He didn't have a choice.

"All right. If you have to see the spot, I guess I can't stop you. But I'll take you."

"That's not—"

"Necessary," he finished for her. "I know. But that's still how it's going to be."

She looked at him as if measuring the depth of his determination. Finally she nodded. "All right. We'll go together."

She'd asked him to help her. He'd agreed. He couldn't turn back now, no matter how convinced he was that she'd just end up hurt by this. And no matter how often he told himself that he ought to stay away from her.

She'd told herself, every time she thought of it, that she didn't need to see the spot where Trevor had died. But when she'd realized no one knew where he'd headed that night, she'd known she had to retrace his steps, no matter how much it hurt.

She gripped the armrest in Nathan's car, trying to think of something to say that wouldn't give away how upsetting she found this. It was good of Nathan to bring her. She shouldn't make him any more uncomfortable than he already had to be.

The road mounted a hill, and her stomach tightened. She looked out the window, trying to concentrate on the view of the lake, its water tinged orange by the setting sun.

Lakemont settled into the curve of the lakeshore

opposite them, its church spire the tallest object in town. From here she could make out the lodge, even the cottage, looking like children's toys set at the edge of the blue lake.

"This road certainly gives you an eagle's-eye view, doesn't it?" She hoped she sounded normal, like any tourist out for a ride to admire the country-side.

He nodded. "Along here it does. Eventually it rounds the curve of the hill, and the lake is out of sight then. That's where the accident happened."

They couldn't avoid the reason that had brought them out here. It was futile to think that.

She clasped her hands in her lap. "Will you tell me about what happened from your perspective?"

A muscle pulsed in his jaw, but he nodded. He was quiet for a moment, as if gathering his thoughts.

"The call came in early in the evening from a motorist with a cell phone." He nodded toward the setting sun. "It was later than this, just about dusk."

She seemed to see the way the road would look in the twilight, with shadows where the surrounding woods were thickest.

"The witness said a car had gone through the guardrail. We called for paramedics, and they got here a few minutes after we did, but it was already too late. There was nothing anyone could have done."

"I know." She swallowed, her throat muscles

tight. "The report we saw said he'd been killed instantly."

Gone in a moment, with no time to say any last words, make any amends for past errors. Still, Trevor had been a person of faith. If he'd known in that split second what was happening, he'd have known that God was with him.

"Witnesses told us he'd swerved to avoid a deer. That happens more often than you'd think. It's dangerous just at dusk, when the deer are moving and hard to see."

She nodded, her hands gripping tightly. She wanted to say this was pointless, that they should go back, but she couldn't. She had to see for herself.

Nathan slowed the car, switched on his flashers and pulled to the side of the road. "That's where it happened, just ahead of us."

She suspected that if she tried to get out of the car, he'd stop her. She didn't need to. The spot where the guardrail had been replaced was evident, the railing still a little brighter there. The hillside fell off steeply beyond it. She tried not to imagine the car plunging down that hill.

I know Trevor is safe in Your hands, Father. Let him be at peace now.

She cleared her throat. "How much farther would it be along this road before you come to anything?"

"The county seat is the next town. About twenty miles. It's roughly twice the size of Lakemont, with a bigger business district. People from Lakemont often go there to shop or eat out.''

''Hotels, too, I suppose.''

He nodded.

''So he could have been intending to spend the night there. Either alone or with someone.''

''He could have.'' Nathan's tone was cautious. ''There could be other explanations, though. Maybe he wanted to see someone on the east side of the lake or he decided suddenly to go home. He could have forgotten about his appointment or intended to call Eric the next morning to cancel.''

He was trying to make her feel better, obviously.

''I'd like to believe that, but it still doesn't explain why he lied about coming here.''

Her view of the hillside blurred suddenly, and she realized her eyes had filled with tears.

Nathan turned toward her, the leather seat creaking as he reached out to touch her shoulder in mute sympathy.

''Sorry.'' She brushed the tears away impatiently. ''I keep trying to make sense of it, but I can't. Sometimes I just feel so angry with poor Trevor. I want to shake him and demand answers.''

''There's no reason to feel guilty about that. Anyone would feel that way.'' He hesitated, as if there was something else he wanted to say and wondered if he should.

''Go on.'' She looked at him. ''Whatever it is you're thinking, just say it.''

"Nothing bad. I just wondered how Trevor felt about the baby."

"He was delirious." Her lips curved at the memory. "I've never seen anyone so excited about the idea of being a father. He ran out at ten o'clock on the night I told him and bought roses for me and a teddy bear for the baby."

"That's a nice memory to hang on to." Nathan's voice was soft.

"He had all sorts of plans for our future as a family—a house with a nice yard, good schools. He wanted to spend more time with his child than his father had with him."

Poor Trevor. He hadn't had a chance to carry out those plans. They'd all ended on this quiet hillside.

Nathan gripped her shoulder. "You know, that doesn't sound like a man who's going off on an illicit weekend with someone else."

"That's what I keep telling myself. But he lied." Her throat tightened. "No matter what problems we might have had, I'd never have believed Trevor would lie to me."

She'd revealed more about her marriage to Nathan than she'd intended to, and she suspected he probably guessed at things she didn't say.

"I wish I could explain that for you. I can't. But I will see Evelyn tomorrow and try to learn something we can go on."

"Thank you, Nathan. I can't tell you how much I appreciate everything you're doing to help."

She turned her face toward him just as he lifted his hand from her shoulder, and his fingers brushed her cheek. A startling wave of longing swept through her, and she had to fight it down.

She wouldn't feel that. She couldn't.

Chapter Eight

Nathan paused in the archway leading to the lodge dining room Friday night, his gaze passing over the small number of weekend check-ins and automatically seeking the person he wanted to see.

And didn't want to see. If he actually tried to explain his feelings to anyone, he'd sound crazy.

He didn't want to hurt Susannah. More than anything else, he didn't want to hurt her.

But he had to tell her what he'd learned—there was no way out of that. No matter what he did, she'd be hurt. He'd known all along this quest of hers would end badly.

Well, there was no point in putting it off. The lodge's dinner guests were filtering out of the room, for the most part. A clatter of dishes from beyond the swinging door said that Rhoda was cleaning up, hopefully with some help from Jen. Susannah sat alone at a small table near the fireplace, nursing a cup of coffee.

No, tea, he corrected automatically. She drank tea. It was one more little fact about Susannah that he was storing away.

She lifted the cup, cradling it in both hands as if enjoying its warmth. She wore her auburn hair loose tonight, and it caught the reflection of the wood fire he'd started earlier, and glinted back answering sparks. She glanced up at his approach, and her face lit.

"Nathan. I didn't realize you were here for dinner tonight." She made an inviting gesture toward the chair opposite her.

Her pleasure wasn't because he was here, he told himself. It was for the information she hoped he had.

"I always try to come in for supper so I can check on Dad. I have to go back on duty soon. Jared and I take turns making sure Friday night doesn't get too rowdy."

Her smile flickered. "It's hard to imagine any night in Lakemont turning rowdy."

"We have our moments." He lifted a hand to Rhoda, who'd come back into the room carrying a tray, and she was there in an instant with coffee for him.

The little exchange gave him a brief respite before he had to talk to Susannah. To tell her. The rest of the guests had left the room. They could talk unheard once Rhoda went into the kitchen.

He glanced back, to find Susannah staring into the fire, her expression pensive. A wave of auburn hair caressed her cheek, and her arm curved gently across her stomach, as if she protected the life within automatically.

To his surprise, that gesture didn't seem to hurt any longer. At some point over the past week he'd stopped looking at Susannah as a reminder of Linda. He saw her only as herself now.

That was a good thing, wasn't it? It should make it easier to deal with her.

Or did it? Those flashes of attraction—well, that happened. He was only human, after all. It didn't have to mean anything.

He'd had his soul mate. He wasn't stupid enough to think that God provided more than one of those in a lifetime. Look what had happened when Dad had tried to manufacture feelings for another woman. They were left with a depleted bank account and a kid who didn't belong here.

Rhoda moved away, beginning to clear tables. Susannah looked at him expectantly.

"Did you have time to speak with the woman at the café today?"

"Yes."

She raised an eyebrow. "Am I going to have to cross-examine you?"

"No, I guess not." She was going to be hurt. He couldn't prevent that. "Like we thought, Evelyn was curious about Trevor. She remembered him coming in. Sounds as if he went there most evenings after he had dinner here. She said he didn't eat anything—just had a cup of coffee.''

"Did the woman talk with him?"

"She tried." He remembered Evelyn's obvious disappointment. "But apparently Trevor didn't respond to her efforts very well. He was polite, she said, but he didn't say much.''

"He would be polite, even if she drove him crazy. Trevor's courtesy was part of him." Susannah studied his face. "What else?"

"She said Trevor always put his cell phone on the table while he drank his coffee." He had to push the words out. "Like he was waiting for a call.''

"I see." Pain flickered in Susannah's eyes, but she quickly masked it, her long lashes sweeping down over any betrayal of feeling. "Did Evelyn notice if he received any calls?''

"Every evening." The words tasted sour in his mouth. "She said he got a call every evening, and then he'd pay his bill and go out.''

Susannah's hands clasped each other tightly on the table, the knuckles white. He quenched a sudden longing to put his hands over hers to comfort her.

She seemed to absorb the same implication he had. Trevor had been meeting someone, clearly. And he'd had to wait for a call before he could go to that meeting. Some obvious reasons that might be the case jumped to mind.

"What else?"

"Nothing," he said, too quickly.

"What is it? I can tell there's more, Nathan." She half rose, her chair scraping back. "I'll go and see her myself, if I have to."

He did reach out to catch her hand then, stopping her. The warmth and smoothness of her skin seemed to imprint itself on his palm, and for a moment he couldn't think. Then he nodded toward Rhoda, still clearing tables nearby.

Susannah sent a frustrated glance toward the woman, but she subsided back into her chair. He had a few moments before Rhoda, apparently sensing Susannah's gaze on her, moved away. It wasn't enough time to come up with an easy way of saying this.

"Evelyn was curious, of course. She knew who Trevor was. She managed to get close enough to overhear a few words." He forced the words out. "She said he was making an appointment to see someone. She heard him say he'd be there soon. That he was only a few minutes away."

Susannah's face was rigid, pressing her emotions down fiercely, as if she didn't dare let them loose. "Did she hear a name?"

"No." He was almost grateful for that.

Coward. You don't want to see her pain when she finds out who it was.

"But apparently she was near enough to Trevor that she says she could hear the response. Not the words, but the timbre of the voice. She claims it was a woman."

Her fingers gripped his hand tightly, as someone in pain would hold on to any available hand like a lifeline. "I suppose I shouldn't be surprised, should I?"

Her pain tightened around his heart. "There might still be some innocent explanation, but—"

"But you don't think so," she finished for him.

"I was going to say that I didn't see any way of finding out." He tried for a cool, professional tone. "For a moment let's assume the worst—that he was here to see some woman in Lakemont. There are a lot of people within a few minutes' walking distance of the café, and a lot more within a few minutes' driving distance. I don't see any way I can find out who he went to visit."

"Maybe not." Her gaze seemed to turn inward. "But I think I can."

"If you're thinking of talking to Evelyn again, you won't get any more. You'll just set her talking." Surely that was the last thing Susannah would want.

"Not Evelyn. Margaret."

He stared at her blankly. "Margaret?"

"Trevor's secretary." She seemed to steady herself, maybe buoyed by having a plan of action. She let go of his hand, pressing her palms on the table. "Don't you see? I never thought of it, but the cell phone he had with him was his business one. The records would go to his secretary. I can get them from her.''

''If the statement is like mine, it won't show calls he received, just ones he made.''

''No, but if he made any calls to that person, the number would be shown. Surely he would have. And then you can find out whose number it is.''

She glanced at her watch. ''Margaret will have left the office by now. I don't want to call her at home. That would make it seem too important. She'd be bound to suspect something. I'll have to wait until Monday morning to reach her.'' Now she clasped his hand, as if to compel his agreement. ''She can fax the records to the office here, can't she?''

Her fingers clung to his, seeming to reach right into his heart and wring it. He gave a reluctant nod.

This would end badly. She'd be hurt, and the way things were going, he would be, too.

He'd never intended to let Susannah get so close. Somehow things had spun out of his control, and he didn't see any way of getting them back to normal again.

Susannah glanced at her watch as she pulled the car up to the front of the lodge on Saturday evening. It was late—later than she'd expected to be returning with Jen from working on the homecoming float. Her lower back ached, and she longed for the comfort of her bed.

But Jen had seemed in a talkative mood when she picked her up, and the girl had been chilled after working on the float in the unheated garage the youth group had borrowed. So Susannah had suggested hot chocolate, and they'd stopped at the café.

The minutes had stretched into an hour as Jen talked and Susannah listened. And tried not to wonder which of the cozy booths Trevor had sat in, waiting for a call every evening.

She now knew a lot more about Jennifer than she'd known before. Certainly more than Nathan knew. But how she could translate that into a better relationship between Jen and Nathan—well, that she didn't know.

It wasn't her business, or her responsibility. The reminder didn't seem to absolve her of the need to try.

"It's later than I thought it was." Jen's hand halted its movement toward the door handle as she looked at the time on the dashboard clock.

This was probably not the right moment to remind Jennifer that Susannah had suggested the girl call to tell Daniel that she'd be late.

"I'll walk in with you," she said casually. "There's something I want to mention to Nathan, if he's here."

Jen's face seemed to stiffen at the name, but she got out and waited while Susannah negotiated the steps. Did Jen feel the need for moral support? That seemed likely.

That need was justified the moment they walked into the hallway. Nathan stood waiting at the bottom of the steps, his face an eloquent storm. Probably only the murmur of voices from the lounge saved them from thunder and lightning.

He took a quick step toward them. Susannah's heart quailed, but his gaze was locked on Jen, not her.

"Where have you been?" The fact that his voice was low didn't disguise the anger in it. "Don't you know how late it is? Why didn't you call?"

Barraging Jennifer with questions wasn't the way to get answers, but she didn't think she'd point that out to Nathan now. She could hear the concern under his anger, but Jen probably didn't.

"Sorry," she put in quickly, before Jen could get out the sharp retort that was undoubtedly on her tongue. "It's my fault. I suggested we stop for hot chocolate, and I'm afraid we lost track of the time."

The look Nathan shot her was annoyed. Clearly he'd prefer her absence to her presence. Well, he wouldn't get his wish this time.

"That's nice of you, but Jen knows it's her responsibility to call if she's going to be late." He frowned at the girl. "Don't you?"

"It's not that late." Jen retreated behind a sulky mask, the lively, interesting face she'd shown to Susannah wiped out in an instant. "Anyway, what do you care?"

"Of course he cares." She got the words in before Nathan could release another clap of thunder. "He was worried about you."

"Oh, yeah?" Jen gave the classic retort. "Well, he sure doesn't act like he was worried."

She cast Nathan an appealing glance. Didn't he hear what she did beneath the girl's sulky tone? Jen wanted to hear him say he cared that she'd been late, because no one else in her life did.

Please, Lord. Let him see what I see.

Nathan's face was as much a mask as Jen's was, but she thought some emotion other than anger flickered in the depths of his eyes.

Please, she thought again, trying not to analyze the reasons this mattered so much to her.

She touched Jen's shoulder, feeling the tension in that thin frame. She moved her hand in reassuring circles, trying to convey comfort.

Nathan needed to say the right thing now. He was the one Jennifer looked to for acceptance, not her.

He let out a long, slow breath, and she seemed to feel his reluctant acceptance of her words across the few feet that separated them.

"Susannah's right." His voice was a low rumble. "I was angry because I was worried. About you."

Jen's lashes fluttered as she glanced up at him. She seemed to be checking to be sure he meant it. Whatever she saw must have reassured her.

"Sorry," she muttered. "Guess I should've called. Susannah said I should, but I thought—" She stopped, then shrugged.

Nathan seemed to hear what she didn't say. His expression softened. "Yeah, well, next time call, okay? My dad was worried, too. He wanted to go out looking for you."

"He did?" For just an instant Jen looked as if he'd handed her a present. She covered the expression quickly with one that suggested boredom, but Susannah had seen it. She only hoped Nathan had, too.

"Maybe you ought to go up and tell him goodnight," Nathan said.

"Yeah, guess I'll do that." Jen sauntered the few steps toward the stairs, then broke into a run, taking the steps two at a time.

Susannah looked from the girl's retreating figure back to Nathan. Her heart gave a little jolt. He was looking at her as if…

No, maybe it was safer not to analyze what his expression meant.

"I should go." She started to turn away, but somehow her hands had become entangled with his.

"How did you do that?" His voice was a baritone rumble that set her nerves tingling.

"Do what?" It certainly was a good thing he couldn't know how that sound affected her.

"Short-circuit the fight we were going to have."

"I just tried to get you to hear each other." She should pull her hands away. She didn't want to.

"You succeeded." Nathan's fingers had begun

moving in slow, mesmerizing circles on her palms, robbing her of thought.

"Well, I…" It took an effort to get her brain into gear. "Jen was being a teenager, you know."

"I know." He frowned. "I just wish somebody who was actually related to her would step forward to take on her teenage troubles. We thought her mother would be back weeks ago."

What exactly was he thinking? "If there were someone suitable, wouldn't Jen's mother have left her with that person to begin with?"

"I suppose." His gaze evaded hers, as if he was sorry he'd brought it up.

It wasn't her business, she reminded herself. "I just hope Daniel wasn't too upset."

His grip tightened on hers. "He gets upset so quickly since the heart attack. It's easy enough for the doctor to tell him not to worry. The doctor's not coping with a teenager. Worry comes with the territory."

Worry. She tried not to think how tempting it was to lean against his broad chest and let her own worries evaporate.

She managed a smile. "And he's got me to cope with, too. I could move into town—"

"No." His voice was soft, for her ears only. "No, you can't. It's too late for that. We already care what happens to you."

A wave of warmth went through her. She should just be glad he'd included Daniel in that declaration.

She should definitely not be longing to hear him say that he was the one who cared about her.

Susannah's pace slowed as she approached the lodge steps on Monday morning. For some reason the shallow stairs looked like Mount Everest to her. The fatigue that had dogged her on Saturday evening had only increased since then, and the baby felt even heavier.

I wish you were here already, little Sarah. I wish I were holding you in my arms.

Or did she? She felt oddly reluctant to move either forward or backward. The fierce need that had driven her since she'd arrived at the lodge had seemed to seep away, leaving her adrift.

Adrift. The word reminded her of Jennifer. Jen floated where she was pushed, an autumn leaf swept by the wind. Nathan's words about another relative taking the girl stuck in her mind like a burr. Was he trying to send her away? Jennifer needed a place to belong, even if that place wasn't with her mother.

Well, she couldn't accept responsibility for Jen. Daniel, it seemed, already had. And as for Nathan...

She fought to push away the warmth that crept through her when she thought of Nathan. Nathan might think he wanted to be free of Jen, but his built-in sense of responsibility was just as great as his father's. He couldn't stop taking care of Jen no matter how much he wanted to.

And what about her? Was that what Nathan felt for her—responsibility? Obligation?

The mere thought ought to offend her, but somehow she couldn't muster up enough energy for that. Maybe this odd indecision was just the fuzzy thinking people said came with pregnancy. She'd rather believe that than think she'd let her feelings for Nathan affect her.

She had to go on to the next thing. She grasped the railing and forced herself up the steps to the lodge. That meant she had to go inside and wait by the fax machine for the truth to come rippling slowly out.

The moment she opened the door Nathan came striding to meet her. Odd how that uniform made him seem even bigger. He didn't really need a badge to look authoritative, though. That, like his sense of responsibility, was built in to his very nature.

"Good morning." He studied her face, as if measuring the circles under her eyes. "You look tired."

She mustered a smile. "If that's supposed to make me feel better, it doesn't."

"Sorry." He clasped her elbow, apparently driven to protect her whether he wanted to or not. "The office is this way."

He led her past the reception desk and through a doorway beyond it. As he closed the door behind them, she glanced around the small office.

Solid mission furniture looked as if it had sat in the same place for a generation or more, and multipaned windows framed in dark wood molding gave a view of the lake. The room might be old-fashioned, but it had an air of permanence that was reassuring.

"Please make yourself comfortable. No one will disturb us here."

"Us?" She lifted her eyebrows. "I thought you were on your way to work."

Nathan pulled out a golden oak desk chair and positioned it near the fax machine that shared space with a printer on a long library table against one wall.

"I don't have to go in right away. I thought I'd wait until you received the information. I assume you've already called."

"You don't need to wait. I don't know how quickly Trevor's secretary will get back to me."

He leaned on the edge of the desk. "I might not need to, but I want to." He gave her a quizzical look. "You asked me to help. Are you having second thoughts?"

"No." She sat down in the chair he'd placed for her. The arms curved comfortably around her, as if inviting her to stay. "I need your help."

"Don't sound so reluctant about it. It's not a crime to need help."

"I know."

But I don't want you to feel responsible for me, Nathan. Because if you do, I might come to depend on that.

He was silent for a moment, as if wondering whether she really accepted that or not.

"When you spoke with Trevor's secretary, did she seem to suspect anything?"

"Not as far as I could tell." She shook her head, trying to concentrate. "Trevor's cousin is running the shipping business now, but Margaret seemed happy to talk to me. I told her I needed to sort out any personal calls Trevor had made. She agreed without asking questions."

Nathan was frowning, and his eyes didn't meet hers. "I just wondered—well, sometimes a secretary might know or suspect more about her boss's activities than she lets on, especially if she's the loyal sort."

"If he were having an affair, you mean." She tried to look at the possibility objectively, as if it were someone else's marriage in question. "I don't think there was any hint of that. Margaret always seemed to have a great deal of respect for Trevor. People did, you know." She couldn't help the challenge in her voice.

"I didn't know him well enough to say." Nathan slid away from confrontation. "You did."

"He was an honorable man." She clung stubbornly to that fact. If it weren't true, if everything she'd thought she knew about Trevor were false, what did that leave her? "I remember how determined he was, when he took over the business after his father died, that people would know they could rely on his word.''

"He doesn't sound like a man who would tell a lie without a very good reason."

"But he did. I just keep coming back to that." She pushed her hair back from her face. "I knew Trevor from the time we were children. I'd have said there wasn't anything I didn't know about him. We were friends."

Friends. Once she'd thought that was the most important thing in a marriage. Now she wasn't so sure. Maybe that friendship hadn't been enough for Trevor.

She shifted in the chair. Somehow it didn't seem so comfortable now. Why was it taking so long for Margaret to respond?

"I suppose all of us have secrets we keep, even from the people who are closest to us."

Did you keep secrets from Linda, Nathan?

That was a question she didn't dare to ask. Nathan had made it clear that his marriage was out of bounds.

"I don't know—"

She stopped. The fax machine had come to life.

Her fingers gripped the curved arms of the chair. Nathan shoved away from the desk and moved to the machine. He glanced at her and nodded.

She ought to get up, but she couldn't seem to move. She could only sit and wait while Nathan pulled the paper from the machine, took two steps toward her and held it out.

A wave of nausea swept over her as she accepted the sheet. Maybe Trevor had never called the woman—the person—from his cell phone. Maybe...

She forced her gaze down the page. She zeroed in on the dates, looking for a Lakemont number. And found it.

She was taking an irrevocable step. There'd be no going back once she knew.

She held the paper out to Nathan. "There it is. Will it take you long to find out whose listing it is?"

Nathan studied the sheet. His face tightened, his level brows drawing down in a forbidding frown. "No." He seemed to force the word out. "It won't take any time at all. I know whose number it is. It's Rhoda's."

Chapter Nine

How could he have been so stupid as to blurt it out like that? When he saw Susannah's stricken face, he wanted to kick himself.

That would hardly help matters now. He bent over her, putting his hand on her shoulder, feeling fragile bone and supple muscle. Tension vibrated from her so strongly he could feel it.

"I'm sorry. I shouldn't have told you that way." He'd known from the start that he wouldn't be any good at this. He couldn't give Susannah what she needed, and he was only making matters worse.

"There wasn't any good way of telling me." The ghost of a smile crossed her face and vanished again. "Stop kicking yourself over it."

Susannah did seem to have a way of knowing what he was thinking.

"Do you want a glass of water?"

She made a faint negative motion in response. "I don't need water. I'm all right."

She didn't look all right, but he didn't think it would help to say so. Her eyes had darkened, and the skin drew tightly across her cheekbones. She seemed to have aged in front of him.

She took a deep breath, as if trying to rally her forces to deal with this blow. She tilted her head back to look at him, her hair floating across his hand like the ripple of wind on the lake.

"You know, Trevor could have called Rhoda for something completely unrelated to the person he visited in the evenings, though."

She moved impatiently, shifting under his hand. "Such as what?"

"I can't think of anything, but—"

"You can't think of anything because there isn't anything." Her mouth was a firm, straight line. "He saw Rhoda every day here at the lodge. If he'd wanted to have some innocent conversation, they could have had it then."

Susannah had gotten a grip on herself now, and she was arguing this painful subject the way she'd argue a case in court. Unfortunately, he could feel how tenuous that control was. He didn't think she'd be able to maintain that detachment for long.

"You don't know that for sure."

She focused on him. "Did you ever see them talking together while he was here?"

He tried to visualize that period. Hopeless. How could he possibly remember?

"Not that I can recall. Rhoda usually keeps to herself. Still, even if I had seen them, I'm not sure I'd have thought anything about it. Rhoda used to work for Trevor's family, after all."

"I haven't forgotten that."

Was she wondering if a relationship had started between Trevor and Rhoda that long ago—one that he'd found a reason to start up again recently?

"Look, do you want to talk to my father about it?" He didn't want to worry his father with this, but he didn't have much choice. "He'd be around more to notice something than I would."

"No." The fine lines around her mouth deepened. "I want to talk to Rhoda."

He tightened his grip on her shoulder. "Wait. Think about this first."

"What is there to think about?" She looked up at him, pain etched on her face. "I have to know."

Her pain seemed to reach out and encompass him, so that his very bones ached with it. But he could see beneath the anguish to the strength of her character. This hurt her unimaginably, but Susannah wouldn't turn back.

Susannah was an honest woman—maybe too honest for her own comfort. He'd seen the doubt in her when she'd talked about her relationship with Trevor. She'd spoken of friendship and respect, not passion.

She was questioning herself, wondering if she was to blame for whatever had led Trevor back to Lakemont. She couldn't stop searching until she knew.

"Yes," he said quietly. "I guess you have to know."

He straightened, releasing his grasp on her shoulder, then held out his hand to her. "Let's go find Rhoda."

"You don't have to—"

"We've already done that bit, haven't we?" He tried to coax a smile. "I'm coming with you."

"In case I fall apart?"

"In case you need a friend to lean on."

He should feel trapped, but he didn't. He tried to analyze his reaction as they went out of the office. Normally he ran like a thief at the thought of an emotional scene. Apparently normal didn't apply in this case.

It took too little time to figure out where Rhoda was. The sound of the vacuum cleaner echoed down the hall from the library.

He watched Susannah straighten and turn toward the sound. He fell into step beside her. She wouldn't turn back, he thought again. If all he could do for her was be there, that was what he'd do.

"Look," he said quietly beneath the noise as they approached the door. "Why not let me take the lead. Rhoda knows me."

For a moment he thought she'd tell him again that

he didn't need to do that. Then she nodded, tension making the movement jerky.

The library was peaceful with the morning sunlight streaming through the windows. The low shelf under the window seat was crammed with the mysteries and cowboy stories he'd loved as a kid; the window seat had been his favorite perch on a rainy day. Today the peace seemed an illusion.

Rhoda, seeing them, switched off the vacuum. She straightened, giving him a questioning look. "Would you like me to finish this later?" She made a tentative movement toward the door.

"No." There was no good way of getting into this. "Sit down, Rhoda, please. We'd like to talk with you."

Rhoda looked from him to Susannah, her face as composed as always. She bypassed the closest seat, an overstuffed armchair, and sat down on a wooden straight-back chair. Folding her hands, she waited for him to speak.

That was Rhoda. Self-contained, self-sufficient, aloof. No one ever seemed to get close to her. The burden of caring for her son must be heavy, but she never let anyone see the weight of it.

For just an instant, as he guided Susannah to a spot on the sofa opposite Rhoda, he thought how odd it was that he sided with a woman he'd known less than a couple of weeks against someone he'd known most of his life.

Maybe it wasn't odd at all. After all these years,

he still didn't understand what made Rhoda tick. But he did understand this much about Susannah. She, just as he did, valued truth at any cost.

The silence was stretching too long, and there was no way to do this but to come right out with it.

"Rhoda, we need some answers from you. We know about Trevor."

There was a flicker of fear in Rhoda's eyes, but she quickly masked it.

"I don't know what you mean." Her mouth tightened, as if to convey offense, but he'd already seen the fear.

"I think you do." He stood over her, deliberately intimidating. The faster this was over, the better. He didn't think Susannah could tolerate much more. "We know Trevor visited you at home in the evenings when he was here. Before he died."

For an instant Rhoda seemed to shrink in the chair. Then she lifted her head, glaring at him defiantly. "Spying on me, were you?"

"No." He hated this. "It's a small town, Rhoda. Someone always knows."

"It's not anyone's business what I do with my free time or who visits me."

That was as good as an admission that they were right, and his heart sank. No happy endings would come from this, just pain.

"It's Susannah's business who her husband saw before he died."

Rhoda's mouth set in a hard line. If she were

pushed into a corner, she'd take refuge in silence, and no one could make her speak.

"Come on, Rhoda. Don't make this harder than it has to be."

She wasn't going to speak. This would all be for nothing. His helplessness galled.

Susannah stood suddenly, leaning toward Rhoda. Her hand moved in a probably unconscious gesture of supplication.

"I have to know the truth. Please. Just tell me the truth. Were you having an affair with my husband?"

The words seemed to set up a vibration in the air. Spoken, they couldn't be taken back.

For a long moment Rhoda didn't move. Then she thrust herself out of the chair.

"This is crazy. You have no right to question me like this, either of you."

"Rhoda—" he began, but she cut him off with a violent shake of her head.

"No right," she repeated. Her face twisted. "But I'll answer you anyway. No, I wasn't having an affair with Trevor. He just stopped by to talk. That's all."

He'd like to believe her. It would be so much easier if he could. But he heard the hollow sound in her denial. Rhoda was hiding something.

"Talk about what?" He asked the question, knowing it was futile.

She spun and was at the door in a few quick steps. "I don't have anything else to say. Am I fired?"

He couldn't force the truth from her. "No, of course not. But—"

She was gone before he could say another word.

He turned toward Susannah. A tremor seemed to go through her, and then she swayed, her face white, hand reaching out blindly for support.

He was next to her in an instant, his arm going around her. He never should have let her go through with this. In her condition she should be protected, not subjected to this sort of trauma.

"Easy, it's all right." He tried to sound more reassuring than he felt.

He half led, half carried her the few steps to the sofa and eased her to a sitting position, then sat beside her. What kind of idiot was he to have let her in for this?

He'd been right all along. There was no way he could possibly give Susannah what she needed.

She'd thought she was ready to know the truth. She'd been wrong. Susannah was vaguely aware that she was clinging to Nathan's hand. She ought to let go, but she couldn't. His strong presence was all that kept her from falling apart.

Please, Father. Help me deal with this.

She took one steadying breath, then another, and managed to look at Nathan. His worried expression enabled her to straighten. She had to at least look as if she were coping, even if that was a lie.

"It's all right," he said again.

She turned toward him, still unable to let go of his hand. "She said she wasn't having an affair with Trevor. I didn't believe her."

"Susannah…"

She tightened her grip. "You've known her a long time. What did you think?"

His fingers were warm and strong on hers. For a moment he didn't meet her gaze, but then he looked in her eyes. She saw his reluctance. He didn't want to hurt her.

"It's all right." She tried to sound as if that were the truth. "You can tell me what you think."

He shook his head slowly. "I don't know. Rhoda has never been easy to read."

"But you have an opinion." Somehow she had to make him say it.

"What she said didn't ring true. She's hiding something. I'm sorry. I wish I felt otherwise, but…" He let that trail off. He didn't need to finish it.

"I know." Tears stung her eyes. "I asked you for the truth. I don't expect you to sugarcoat it."

"There's nothing sugarcoated about this." His grip tightened. "I'm sorry."

"I wish I could at least pretend I believed her, but I can't."

"Maybe after Rhoda's had a chance to think about it, I can get her to open up a little more. But that's not going to make you feel any better."

"No, I guess not." She tried to swallow, but the lump in her throat made it almost impossible. "I thought I was ready to accept this, whatever it was, but now—''

Her voice broke, and that wasn't the only thing that was broken. She felt as if she were flying apart. She might never be able to put herself together again.

She tried to speak, but all that came out was a strangled sob. She couldn't cry. She never cried in front of anyone, not even Trevor, and she'd known him all her life. But Nathan's arms had gone around her, and the tears she'd tried so hard not to shed began to flow.

''I can't—''

''It's all right.'' He held her against him. ''It's all right. You can cry. Anyone would.''

She should be strong. But she just couldn't. She let the misery sweep over her, let the sobs rack her body. She was conscious of nothing but the harsh sound of her weeping and the pain that struck deep into her soul.

After what seemed like a very long time the sobs began to lessen, as if she'd cried all she had to cry. Her breath still came in little choking sobs, but she was aware again of the quiet, warm room, the ticking of the clock.

No. The warmth wasn't from the room—it was from Nathan's arms around her. The sound wasn't a clock, but the steady beating of his heart against her cheek.

She pulled back, confused, trying to mop her eyes. She shouldn't have let this happen.

"I'm sorry." She barely managed the words. "That was…such a cliché. The pregnant woman, crying."

Given Nathan's history, she'd expect him to be running for cover. Instead he was as solid as the mountain.

"You have a right to cry. Anyone would." His voice was a low, unembarrassed rumble. "Even I might."

She shook her head, smiling a little. Nathan wouldn't. But then, Nathan's love had been true to him.

She felt vainly in the pockets of her jumper. "Wouldn't you know I don't have a tissue when I need one?"

He pulled a folded handkerchief from his pocket. Instead of handing it to her, he wiped her cheeks gently, as if she were a child who required comforting. His touch was too disarming, setting her heart thumping.

"You don't need…" She reached for the handkerchief, her fingers entangling with his.

"I know I don't." His voice was so soft it was barely a breath, and his fingertips stroked her cheek.

Every cell of her body seemed to respond to that touch, and a flood of warmth swept over her. She met his eyes, startled and shaken. Somehow, in that moment, their hearts were open to each other.

She'd never know whether she moved toward him or he moved toward her. In an instant they were kissing.

She was lost again, this time in the power of the emotions that surged between them. His arms were strong and protective around her, keeping her safe. She touched his shoulder, then the sturdy column of his neck, wanting to be even closer. This was what she wanted, this longing, this tenderness, this passion.

Nathan pulled away from her with an abrupt movement. He looked shocked, confused. For an instant longer her hands clung to him, and then she clasped them together, mortified, trying to gain control of herself.

He didn't want this. Had she thrown herself at him, in those moments when he was the only anchor in an unstable world? How humiliating. No wonder he looked shocked.

She had to say something, do something to make this right between them. "I'm sorry." She managed to get the words out. "That was my fault."

"No. No, it was mine. I didn't mean for that to happen."

Now he looked ready to run, and all she could do was try to make it easy for him to escape.

"Emotion got the better of me. Let's just forget it." She grasped the arm of the sofa, starting to lever herself up. She had to get out of there before she embarrassed herself any further. "I'd better—"

A gasp cut off the words. Pain, sharp and terrifying, shot through her, obliterating every thought.

Nathan veered the police cruiser into the street leading to the hospital emergency-room entrance, tires squealing as he took the turn. He'd called ahead, so they should be ready for—

He'd almost let himself think, *Linda. They should be ready for Linda.*

No. That was the past. This was now, with Susannah sitting white-faced next to him, clutching her side.

"How are you doing?" He forced himself to sound calm and in control. He couldn't let Susannah guess how helpless he felt in the face of her pain.

She tried to smile, but it didn't work. "It still hurts, but it's better when I'm not moving."

He pulled up at the double doors, letting out a whine on the siren to alert the staff. A wheelchair pushed by two attendants had arrived at the curb by the time he'd raced around the cruiser to open the door.

Susannah looked afraid to move. Her hand groped for his, and he took it, clasping her fingers gently as they transferred her to the wheelchair. When she was safely in place, he could breathe again.

He started to draw away, but her fingers tightened on his, nailing him to her side. Her green eyes were wide and frightened. For her baby—he knew her well enough to guess that.

"Aren't you coming in?"

No.

"Yes. As soon as I park the car." He patted her hand as he detached himself from her grasp. "They'll take good care of you. Don't worry."

Coward.

He pulled into the first available space, ignoring the Staff Only sign. All he wanted to do was run, as far and as fast as possible. He couldn't do Susannah any good, and she'd certainly be better off if she didn't count on him.

But he couldn't run, obviously. He cut the engine and forced himself out of the car. He could only go inside, praying that she was already under the doctor's care.

A knife twisted in his stomach. He could also hope his prayers did more good for Susannah than they had for Linda.

Marge Wilson, the E.R. receptionist, greeted him with a reassuring smile. "The doctor's already with her. You just sit down and relax, Chief."

The perils of small-town life, he thought, remembering what he'd said to Rhoda. Everyone knew his history. Marge had probably even been on duty the day they'd brought Linda in, although he didn't remember. He'd been too focused on Linda to notice anything else.

Sit down and relax. Marge had to be kidding. She probably said that to everyone, and she probably didn't expect anyone to take that advice any more than he could.

He paced the length of the room, turned and paced back again. Beige, everything was beige—the walls, the tile, the fabric on the chairs. Even the magazine rack screwed into the wall was beige. Above his head a television chattered, mindless background noise for anyone who waited.

He was the only one in the waiting room, which should mean that Susannah had the total attention of the on-duty staff. He swung for another circuit of the room and realized that Marge was watching him with ill-concealed pity on her face.

He forced himself to walk to a chair, sit down and pick up a magazine. He wouldn't make it that easy for her to feel sorry for him.

Fifteen excruciatingly slow minutes later he'd paged through the magazine without remembering a thing that was on any page. He let it drop to the seat next to him. Maybe he should do something, call someone.

Maybe he should call Enid. Surely Susannah's mother-in-law should be told if something was wrong.

He could imagine Susannah's reaction to that. *I don't need your help.* But she did need help, like it or not. If the doctor didn't come out soon...

The door swung open. The doctor came through, her face grave as she looked down at a chart in her hands. Angela Morris. He should have realized they'd call the only obstetrician in town.

She'd been Linda's doctor. She'd been the one to tell him about Linda.

Now she was going to tell him about Susannah.

Chapter Ten

Nathan's stomach clenched as he walked toward the doctor. "What's happening? Is Susannah all right?"

She looked at him, then smiled. "You can see for yourself."

Angela reached back to hold the door open behind her. An orderly pushed Susannah, still in a wheelchair, through the door. The vise that had been holding his chest released, and he could breathe again.

"Are you okay?"

"I'm fine." Susannah's smile was a bit strained, but at least she was smiling.

"Nothing to worry about." Angela looked as if she assessed his emotional state and came to her own conclusions. "You can drive our patient back to the lodge now. She's going to be fine."

Susannah seemed to take pity on him for all the

things the doctor didn't say. "Dr. Morris says there's nothing to be concerned about. The baby is just in a position where she's pressing on a nerve. That was what caused the pain."

Apparently released from whatever confidentiality concerns she felt by Susannah's telling him, Angela nodded.

"It happens." She smiled. "I know. That's easy for me to say. But the baby will probably shift again soon, and the pain will ease up."

"What's she supposed to do in the meantime?" That came out more sharply than he intended.

"Just remember what I said." The doctor addressed Susannah, not him. "Bed rest as much as possible for a couple of days."

Susannah wasn't going to like this, but he had to say what was on his mind. "Shouldn't she go back to Philadelphia and see her own doctor?"

Susannah's eyes sparked, but before she could speak, Angela intervened.

"I wouldn't recommend traveling until this eases off. Sitting in a car for several hours would be pretty miserable at this point." The doctor's voice was firm. "Just take Susannah back to the lodge and make sure she stays off her feet."

Angela was acting as if he was responsible for Susannah. He didn't want that. Susannah didn't want that. But they were both stuck for the moment.

"Right." He looked from Angela to the stormy

expression in Susannah's eyes. "I'll pull the car up," he said, and headed for the door.

Once outside, he took a deep breath, trying to rid his lungs of hospital air. He suspected Susannah needed a breathing space to deal with this just as much as he did.

He took his time getting to the car and pulling up to the curb again. By the time the orderly had Susannah settled in the front seat of the cruiser, she seemed to be recovering her poise.

"I'm sorry." She fastened the safety belt carefully and then leaned back against the headrest. "For taking you on this false alarm run, I mean."

The attendant closed the door and patted the roof, as if to say they should stop blocking the E.R. door.

"It wasn't a false alarm. You were in pain." He put the car in gear and pulled slowly out the curving drive.

But it probably would have been better if almost anyone else had taken her to the hospital. Anyone else wouldn't be fighting this gut-crunching mix of grief and guilt at the experience.

"I know. But..." She seemed to think better of whatever she'd been about to say. "Well, I am all right. You know the old saying—it only hurts when I laugh. Well, it only hurts when I move."

"That's a good reason to follow the doctor's orders and stay in bed."

"I'm sure I'll be fine."

Susannah sounded as if she were trying to pull

control back into her own hands. He could hardly blame her for that, but under the circumstances, she had to have assistance, like it or not.

He forced his mind onto practicalities, away from emotion. He could do this if he just didn't think too much. Or feel too much.

"We'll move you into a room at the lodge. Don't worry, we'll take care of everything. You don't have to do anything but stay off your feet, like the doc said."

"My things are all at the cottage. I don't need to move. I'll be fine there."

"No, you won't be fine. You can't stay off your feet if you're alone there."

Alone. The way Linda had been.

He forced that thought away. "I'll have—" He'd almost said Rhoda. That wouldn't work. "I'll have Jen bring you whatever you need." He frowned. "And for once will you please not argue about it?"

He darted a glance at her. She didn't look offended at the blunt words. Her gaze rested on her clasped hands. Then she looked at him.

"All right." She managed a smile. "Since you put it so graciously."

"Guess I'm too worried to be polite." He let the truth come out. "You scared me."

"I'm sorry."

He shook his head. "You don't need to be sorry. It happened. It wasn't your fault."

She hesitated. "Well, I know it had to remind you of your own grief."

Grief. The concept reverberated in his mind. If what he felt were only grief, it might almost be bearable.

"It's not grief." The words came out before he realized he was going to say them. "It's not grief. It's guilt. It's my fault Linda and the baby died."

Nathan's words reached out and wrapped themselves around Susannah's heart, constricting it painfully. She was beginning to learn a thing or two about how guilt felt.

"Nathan…" What could she say to him? Whatever it was, it couldn't be a facile dismissal of the depths of his emotion, not when he'd finally revealed something of himself to her. "Do you want to talk about it?"

"No." He snapped the word out.

Then, as if denying he'd said it, he turned the car into the parking lot at the marina. He pulled to an abrupt halt in a space looking out on the water.

On this late autumn weekday the lot stood empty. A few birds fluttered around the wire trash baskets, and a few boats rocked silently at their places along the dock.

No one was around now. As Nathan had told her, seemingly a long time ago, the parade of leaf watchers trailed off in late October, leaving the village and the lake to itself.

He switched off the ignition, then sat staring at his hands, gripping the wheel. His face was a tight mask, holding pain in, holding her out.

Please, Lord. I don't know what guilt tortures Nathan, and I don't know what I can do. Please help him to speak. Help me to answer with Your words.

"It's not you," he said finally. "It's not your fault that you remind me."

"You don't have to feel responsible for me," she said carefully, choosing her words as if the slightest misstep would be fatal. "And you don't have to tell me. But I think you should talk to someone about this."

His grip seemed to tighten, if that were possible. "So they can tell me it wasn't my fault? Thanks, I've heard that already, plenty of times. But the truth is, Linda wouldn't have died if I'd been there."

Here, at least, was familiar ground. Her own heart ached with it.

"After I found out how Trevor died, I kept thinking the same thing. If I'd been with him, maybe he wouldn't have been distracted. Maybe he wouldn't have been driving so fast. Maybe he'd still be alive." Her voice thickened with pain. "I shouldn't have been out to dinner with friends, laughing and talking, when he was lying on a dark hillside with his life seeping out of him."

Something—either her words or her emotion—seemed to break through the shell he'd put around himself. He reached out to clasp her hand strongly.

"You can't let yourself think that way. You couldn't have known."

She put her other hand over his, holding it securely between hers. "Doesn't the same thing apply to you?"

"No." He tried to pull free, but she held on.

"Why not?"

"It's not the same. You didn't even know Trevor was here. What happened to him was an accident."

"You couldn't have known about Linda's heart condition. Your father said no one knew."

His face was hard, rejecting her sympathy. "I knew she didn't feel well that morning. I should never have gone to work and left her."

She could imagine the scene so clearly. "From what I remember of Linda, she probably laughed it off and told you to go to work."

"Yes." The lines in his face seemed to carve themselves more deeply. "That's just what she did, but I should have known better."

Didn't he realize how futile that was? He would in an instant if it were someone else.

"You couldn't. Nathan, you couldn't have known. Linda wasn't aware of her heart problem, and neither was the doctor. You can't blame yourself for that."

He shook his head, turning away from her. "Leave it alone, Susannah. There's nothing you can say that will make me forgive myself."

"For not being a superman? For not knowing

what the doctor didn't? That doesn't make any sense.''

Lord, he's hurting so much. Please help him. I can't get through to him.

He swung to face her then, and she wasn't sure whether the bitter accusation in his eyes was for himself or for her.

''Maybe not.'' He threw the words at her. ''But I can blame myself for not coming back when I said I would. I didn't come, and she and the baby both died.''

She struggled to find her way through his pain. ''You must have had a reason.''

Duty. It would have been duty—she knew that much about him.

''Not a good enough one.'' He brushed it away. ''There was an accident investigation. I let myself focus on that. I didn't even think to call her.'' His face twisted with pain. ''Do you understand? I didn't even think about her. And when I finally did, it was too late. I lost them both. I can never forget that.''

He turned bleakly inward, his face a mask that shut her out.

She longed to comfort him, but she didn't know how. Nothing she said could make him feel any different, because he couldn't be reached.

She couldn't heal his pain, any more than he could heal hers. They were both lost.

* * *

Susannah walked cautiously across the cozy bedroom at the lodge that she'd occupied for the past two days. There was no recurrence of that scary pain, thank heaven. She patted her stomach.

Thank you, little Sarah. I'm glad you moved. Mommy couldn't have taken much more of that.

Her physical pain had vanished, but the emotional pain remained. She couldn't pretend any longer that there was an innocent explanation for Trevor's lies. She paused by the curved-front oak dresser, looking at the small, heart-shaped frame containing their wedding picture.

What happened, Trevor? What drew you to Rhoda?

Jen had brought the photo from the cottage, along with whatever clothing and toiletries Susannah needed. She'd hustled back and forth, no longer bothering to pretend that being helpful bored her.

For two days Jen had been the one to ask what she needed, to hurry in and out with books and magazines to distract her. She'd set up the television so Susannah could see it easily from the bed.

It had been Jen or Daniel who'd carried up her meal trays, always brightened with a flower in a small vase. Well, she could hardly expect that Rhoda would want to come near her. As for Nathan...

The same applied to Nathan. He'd made his feelings clear by staying completely away from her. She could hardly blame him. He was in pain, and her presence intensified that pain. She hadn't been able to help him.

He doesn't need anything from me, Father. But I think he needs Your help. He has to forgive himself for what happened when Linda died.

She couldn't do anything about Nathan, other than pray for him. And the feelings she had for him had to be buried out of sight—the sooner the better.

As for the rest of it, she could try to talk with Rhoda again, but what good would it do? And how would knowing any more about Rhoda's relationship with Trevor ease the pain in her heart?

Failure, she knew that now. The pain was failure. With the best intentions in the world she and Trevor had failed each other. They hadn't loved the way two people should love in order to be bound together in God's sight. She'd let him down, and he'd taken refuge in lies.

"Hey, you're up. Are you supposed to be?" Jen hovered in the doorway.

"As long as I feel all right, the doctor says it's okay for me to walk around a little." She glanced at her watch. "Why aren't you in town working on the float? Homecoming is almost here."

Jen shrugged, coming into the room and flopping down on the bed. "Nobody to take me. It's okay."

"I'm sorry I can't drive you after I promised." She sat down next to the girl.

"It's not your fault. You have to take care of little Sarah."

"What about Daniel?" Or Nathan, she wanted to ask, but didn't trust herself to say his name normally.

"I didn't want to ask him, because Nathan makes such a fuss every time Daniel wants to drive the car. He thinks he shouldn't." She frowned, clasping both hands around her knees. "Guess Nathan thinks his father would be better off if I'd just go away."

Perhaps that was the truth, but Susannah felt convinced in her own mind that this was one occasion when a lie was justified, even necessary.

"I'm sure he doesn't think that." She put her arm around Jen's thin shoulders. "He just worries about his father's health, that's all. Sometimes worry makes people say things they don't mean."

Jen stiffened, as if to reject Susannah's soft words.

"Yeah, well, I probably won't be around here much longer, anyway. My mother's bound to come for me soon and take me back to Chicago. When she comes, I won't waste any time saying goodbye to this hick town, believe me."

Did Jen really believe her mother was going to reappear soon? Nothing Daniel or Nathan had said indicated they thought so. Her heart ached for the girl.

"Won't there be anything you'll miss?" She tried for a light tone. "Like me, for instance?"

"Yeah, I'll miss you. But you won't be here, either, will you?"

"I guess not." She couldn't do anything else here. It was time to say goodbye to the hope that had brought her. "If the doctor says it's all right, I'll probably leave in the next couple of days."

Jen jerked upright, looking at her with what might almost be a plea in her eyes. "You aren't leaving before the homecoming parade Friday night, are you? If I'm actually going to ride on that stupid float, it'd sort of be nice if you could see me."

"I wouldn't miss it for the world." Maybe she couldn't do anything else for Jen, but she'd do this one thing. She'd watch the parade go by and cheer for her riding on the float. "I have my camera, and I'm going to take lots of pictures."

"Pictures of what?"

She hadn't heard Nathan's voice in two days. It still set up a reverberation inside her, as if they were somehow in tune with each other.

She managed a smile as she glanced at him, standing in the doorway. She wouldn't let him guess at her misery. That would only make him feel more responsible.

"Of Jennifer on the float, of course. I'm looking forward to the homecoming parade."

His eyes expressed a little skepticism at that, but he nodded. "Well, it seems to me if Jennifer's going to ride on the float, she ought to be doing her bit by working on it tonight."

Jen eyed him warily. "I don't have a ride."

"You do now. Go get your jacket. I'll take you."

Jen's face lit up, and she bolted off the bed. "You mean it? Really? I'll be ready in two seconds." She dashed out of the room.

Nathan watched her go, and then shook his head. "It'll take longer than that." He took a cautious step into the room, as if he didn't want to get too close. "She'll have to change her clothes a couple of times. I think there's someone working on the float she wants to impress."

"What makes you think that?" At least he was talking to her again.

"Just a hunch. Believe it or not, I haven't totally forgotten what it's like to be fifteen. I just hope he's a decent kid, whoever he is."

"You're doing a good thing by taking her. It's important to her."

He shrugged. "I'm trying." He moved a step toward the window, holding the curtain aside to glance out the small panes at the sunset's reflection on the lake. "I wanted to tell you I'm sorry."

She got up a little unsteadily, clutching the bedpost. "You don't have anything to be sorry for."

"Yes, I do." He turned slightly, so that he was silhouetted against the red glow of sunset beyond the window. "I unloaded on you when you were dealing with enough trouble of your own. I made you feel responsible, and that's not fair. My feelings aren't your problem."

But they are. They can't help but be, because I care about you.

She couldn't say that. It would just make matters worse between them.

"Look, this situation isn't really anyone's fault." She struggled to express herself in a way that wouldn't hurt either of them. "When I came here, I couldn't know that I was the last person in the world you'd want to be around. And you couldn't know that—"

She stopped. Maybe it was better not to say the rest of it.

"Couldn't know what?" He covered the space between them, and his nearness took her breath away.

"You couldn't know that seeing how powerful your feelings were for Linda made me realize just how weak my marriage was."

He looked stunned for an instant, then shook his head. "You don't mean that. You and Trevor loved each other. Even if he got involved with Rhoda, it doesn't change that."

She swallowed, feeling the lump in her throat. "We loved each other as friends. I think we both wanted someone to belong to so much that we tried to make believe that was a solid foundation for marriage. Trevor just discovered how wrong that was first."

"I'm sorry." His eyes went dark with distress, and he took her hands in his. "I'm sorry for all of it."

She tried to say something, but she couldn't. He

might as well be grasping her heart instead of her hands.

Because she'd done the unthinkable. She'd fallen in love with a man who would probably never be able to love again.

Chapter Eleven

Nathan checked his stride as he walked into the breakfast room the next morning. Susannah sat at her favorite table near the fireplace, her head bent slightly as if she studied the pattern of the china. Autumn sunlight slanted through the windows on either side of the fireplace, lying in a broad swath across her table.

Susannah's bronze hair was tied at the nape of her neck, but a few strands had come loose to curl against her cheek. The soft curve of her still body struck him with a sense of her vulnerability. She wouldn't want to be told that, but Susannah needed someone to stand by her.

But not him. He had nothing left to offer Susannah or anyone else, and certainly not her baby. He couldn't try to cobble a family together out of separate pieces. That way lay disaster.

His father had tried it, and look how badly that had turned out. They were still trying to recover from the aftershocks of that experiment.

Susannah would leave Lakemont in two days, and that was best for both of them. She'd go back to her home in Philadelphia, where she'd have the support of Enid and probably dozens of friends.

She'd have her baby, and gradually the pain of Trevor's loss and his betrayal would fade to a flicker of memory. Susannah would have the life she was meant to have.

And he'd stop letting his gaze automatically search for her every time he entered a room. He'd gotten entirely too involved with Susannah, but life would go back to normal once she was gone.

It would be as if she'd never been here. As if she'd never twisted his heart with her courage or annoyed him with her persistence. He'd forget.

He hoped.

He reached the table. An errant ray of sunlight touched her hair, turning the bronze to flame.

She looked up at him, and his heart contracted. He hadn't seen that expression in her eyes before, and he had to search a moment before he could identify it.

Resignation. Susannah the crusader looked as if she'd given up.

"Good morning." His greeting seemed hollow in the face of her pain.

Well, resignation was natural, wasn't it? She'd

learned the painful truth she'd come to Lakemont in search of. Now she had to figure out how to live with it.

"Good morning." She seemed to rouse herself to gesture to the seat opposite her. "Please join me. Have you had breakfast yet?"

He'd be better off to give her a brief greeting and leave, but he knew he wasn't going to do that. "I've already eaten, but I will have a cup of coffee with you."

He slid into the chair, then gestured across the room, catching Rhoda's eye. She approached with the coffeepot, her steps a bit slower than usual.

He had been so preoccupied with Susannah's physical health and his own emotions that he hadn't spared much thought for Rhoda—and how awkward this situation had to be for her and Susannah.

Susannah stared at her own cup while Rhoda poured his coffee. Once the woman had moved away again, she managed a small smile.

"I see what you mean about the vanishing guests. Everyone is gone."

She gestured around the empty dining room. Several of the round tables had already been stripped and pushed against the walls, leaving an expanse of bare floor.

He nodded. "Just like magic. Once mid-October is past, Lakemont settles into its winter routine."

"You don't move out of the lodge, do you?"

Apparently they were going to talk about the

lodge. Well, he couldn't blame her for wanting to keep the conversation on neutral topics. They'd gotten too far beyond each other's barricades for comfort every time they'd talked in the past few days.

"No, this is home. We just close off the rooms we don't use, so we don't have to heat them. Then we rattle around in the rest."

"There's certainly plenty of space for you to rattle around in."

Was she thinking they'd be lonely? "I guess it might seem funny to some people, but we're used to the routine. When I was a kid, I loved it when everyone left." He smiled at the memory. "My friends and I could play hide-and-seek through the whole place."

"I should think you'd have played cops and robbers instead." She sketched a tiny gesture toward his uniform and badge.

"Well, maybe that, too." He took a gulp of the hot black coffee. "The past few years it's just been Dad and I holed up in here, playing chess in front of the fire." Maybe that did sound lonely.

She studied him for a moment, and he couldn't tell what she was thinking. "This year Jen will be part of the mix, won't she?"

Jen. The weight of the problem she presented rolled back at him.

"I don't know." He frowned down at his mug. "We never expected Jen would be here as long as she has been."

"What does her mother say?"

"Nothing. We haven't heard anything at all from her mother, and neither has Jen. We don't even know where the woman is."

Susannah made a soft sound of dismay. "That's terrible for Jennifer."

He set his cup down so hard the coffee sloshed. "Because we aren't related to Jen, we don't even have the right to seek treatment for her if she should get sick."

She put her hand on the front of her maternity sweater as if reminded of the new life for which she was responsible. Or maybe she was thinking about what she'd do if this were one of her cases.

"Her mother sounds like the kind of person who should be forbidden to have children."

"That's about the size of it. We don't have any rights where Jen is concerned, but if she gets into trouble while she's here—"

He stopped, but not soon enough.

"What kind of trouble?"

When he didn't answer, Susannah's eyebrows rose.

"Something happened last night when you took her to work on the float, didn't it?"

He shot her a half annoyed, half amused look. "Reading minds, are you?"

"You're too easy when it comes to Jen. Come on, you might as well tell me what happened. Did she wear too many earrings?"

"Actually, that I'm used to." He sobered. "No, it wasn't anything like that. I just didn't like the company she was keeping."

"A boy?"

"Of course a boy." He grimaced, remembering how he'd felt when he saw who had his arm around Jennifer. "Most boys I could handle, but this particular kid is trouble."

Her eyes darkened with concern. "He's been in trouble with the law?"

"Not yet," he said grimly.

Susannah drew back a little. "That sounds as if you're prejudging him."

She didn't understand, obviously. Why should she? She hadn't grown up in a place like Lakemont.

"Look, this is a small town. I know the people, including the kids who are looking for trouble and are going to find it, sooner or later. And I know Thad Ferguson isn't someone Jen should be hanging around."

Susannah's face expressed caring. For Jen? For him? He didn't know.

"Maybe Jennifer sees something in him that you don't," she suggested.

He frowned. "Is that Jen's friend speaking, or the family services attorney?"

"A little of both, I guess."

"Just take my word for it." He didn't know why he would imagine she'd do that. She hadn't taken his word for anything so far, on any subject. "Jen will be better off if she stays away from Thad Ferguson."

Susannah lifted one eyebrow in a silent comment. "I suppose you told her so."

"Of course I did." The implication that he'd handled the situation badly nettled him. "I certainly wasn't going to ignore it."

Susannah's gaze seemed to probe beneath his surface, looking for motives. "Would it surprise you to be told you're acting like a big brother?"

He couldn't repudiate that fast enough. "I'm not a relative of Jen's, and having me for a big brother is the last thing she'd want. But I can't help being responsible for her while she's here. That's all there is to it."

"Of course." The faint smile that lingered on her lips suggested she didn't buy that.

He had a feeling arguing about it would be futile. Susannah didn't understand the depth of his feelings about family.

"Well, maybe her mother will turn up soon. Then Jen's friends will be her problem. If she doesn't..." He paused, frowning. Wondering. "Well, then we'll have to look for another solution."

He shouldn't have said that much. He didn't really want to tell Susannah what he'd been thinking.

"What are you going to do if the mother doesn't show up?"

"I'm not sure." That was honest, at least. He really wasn't sure what he intended to do about the situation. "I did some checking to see if any of her mother's relatives could take Jen, but I didn't have any luck."

"Luck?" Her voice rose, her expression suggesting that he'd just said something off-color. "It's not a question of luck to talk about farming that girl out to anyone who would take her."

He should have realized that Susannah, with her history, wouldn't sympathize. He shouldn't have said a word about his attempts to find a place for Jen.

"I was just checking into it."

"Can you imagine how Jen would feel if she knew that's what you were doing?"

Maybe not, but he knew what Susannah was doing. She was putting herself in Jennifer's place, remembering what that felt like.

"Look, nothing came of my inquiries, so you don't have to jump down my throat. I'm just trying to do what's right for the kid."

"Are you?"

He frowned, stung. "You're a professional. You can't think two single men make appropriate guardians for a teenage girl."

"Don't you mean family for her?"

"Not family." The words came out without thought. "You can't put a family together like that. Families are born, not cobbled together from separate pieces."

She recoiled, as if his words had stung her. "That's a pretty harsh judgment."

"It's what I feel." Susannah might be disappointed in him, but he couldn't change what he felt. "In any event, Jen doesn't seem to have any relatives who can take her, so I guess she'll be here until her mother reappears."

"And then you'll have all your difficult females off your hands, won't you?" Susannah's tart tone was tinged with a little sadness.

She meant herself, and he was sorry again that he'd drifted into discussing the subject of Jennifer. He touched her hand lightly.

"I'm not trying to get rid of you."

"No. I appreciate that." She wrapped her arms around herself, as if cold. "But it's time for me to leave. There's nothing else I can do here."

"You're satisfied that you know the truth."

The words sounded so final. He couldn't help wishing—well, what? He already knew that her leaving was best for all of them.

She straightened, hands clasping each other on the table, as if determined to face this bitter truth alone.

"I'll never know how it came about, but I've accepted the fact that Trevor must have been having an affair with Rhoda."

The clatter of a falling tray punctuated her words. He swung around. Rhoda stood a few feet away, staring at them. Her eyes were wide and staring.

"No! I already told you. That's not true!"

Susannah's breath caught at the sight of the woman. She hadn't heard her, but she should have realized by now that Rhoda moved soundlessly.

She pressed her clenched hands against the white tablecloth. The last thing she felt ready for was another encounter with the woman, but it didn't look as if she had a choice. And she wouldn't be a coward.

"I know that's what you told us." She was surprised by how level her voice sounded. "But your denial wasn't very convincing."

Rhoda swung an angry, baffled stare from her to Nathan, shaking her head.

Nathan stood, one hand on the tabletop. Taking charge, of course. He would. She discovered it was easier to focus on his strong hand than on Rhoda's face.

"I've known you for a long time, Rhoda," he said quietly. "I could tell you were hiding something. There's no point in denying the truth any longer."

"But it's not the truth." Rhoda's voice rose, and for the first time her face showed emotion. "I tell you, I never had an affair with Trevor."

The ring of sincerity in her voice startled Susannah. That almost sounded as if she meant it.

She glanced at Nathan. His brows drew down as if he weighed the woman's words.

"Then what are you hiding?" He shot the question at Rhoda like a cop questioning a suspect. But then, why wouldn't he? He was a cop. "Why did he come to see you?"

Rhoda's mouth tightened. Her skin seemed to draw against the fine bones of her face until it almost looked like a death mask.

"I didn't have an affair with Trevor." Saying the words again seemed to give her the strength to go on. "I had an affair with his father." Her hand moved, groping as if for support. "Thomas is his son."

The quiet words rattled through Susannah's mind, ricocheting against the things she thought she knew, rearranging them until at last they fell into a pattern that made some kind of sense.

"Franklin Laine," she said numbly. The father Trevor had idolized.

"Yes." Rhoda's mouth twisted. "The great man himself, having an affair with a maid in his house. Having a child by her."

She swayed suddenly, as if telling them had taken her last vestige of strength. Before Susannah could move, Nathan had grasped Rhoda's arm and piloted her to a chair.

Poor Nathan. He was being let in for yet another emotional scene. He probably wanted to run, but he didn't show any signs of fleeing.

"Did Franklin know about Thomas?" He put the question quietly.

"No. I never wanted them to know, any of them." She shot Susannah a look that seared. "I never wanted to have anything more to do with the Laines.''

"But you did," Nathan said. "At some point you got in touch with Trevor."

Nathan seemed to be putting this together faster than she was. He was figuring out what must have happened while she still stumbled through accepting it.

Little though she wanted to involve him further, she was grateful. She couldn't seem to get her mind around all of it yet.

Rhoda looked up at Nathan, then nodded. "Yes. I wrote to Trevor and told him."

As if aware that he was looming over her, Nathan pulled his chair closer to Susannah's and sat down. That unspoken gesture of support, aligning himself with her, seemed to give her strength.

"When did you write to him?" She finally put a question. How long had Trevor withheld this secret from her?

Rhoda rubbed her forehead. "I don't know. March, maybe. It was after Thomas had that long siege with bronchitis last winter, and then I caught the flu. It made me think about what would happen to him if anything happened to me." Sudden fire colored her cheeks. "That's all it was. I wanted to be sure Thomas was protected if something happened to me."

"We understand." Nathan's voice was gentle, encouraging her to continue. "You were just trying to take care of your boy."

"So Trevor came to see you about it in March, after you got in touch with him." That explained Trevor's brief earlier visit.

And he didn't tell me anything about it but a lie. Why, Lord? Why didn't he tell me?

Rhoda nodded. "Trevor understood, once I talked to him about it. I don't think he was even surprised when the DNA test proved it."

Of course Trevor would have insisted on a test. He always wanted to do everything correctly, even handling his father's indiscretion.

"After he saw the test, Trevor said he had to do some checking about how best to handle things so Thomas would be taken care of. Then he'd come back, he said, and we'd make arrangements."

Conscientious Trevor, trying to do what was right, not wanting to let anyone down. "That's why he came here in April. Why he was meeting with you in the evenings."

"I didn't want him to come to the house until after Thomas was asleep." Rhoda said it as if it were the most natural thing in the world. "And we didn't want to meet anywhere else. People might talk."

As, of course, people had talked. Nathan had been right. Not much escaped people in a small town—someone would always see something. The only surprise was that no one seemed to have suspected a long time ago who Thomas's father was.

Her head was throbbing. She wanted nothing more than to be alone to sort this all out, but she had to have all the answers first. "What did Trevor agree to do for your son?"

His brother. Thomas was his half brother. Of course Trevor had accepted the responsibility.

"He was setting up a trust fund to take care of Thomas." Rhoda's hands twisted together. "He had it all figured out, how to provide for Thomas, what to do if something happened to me. He said we had to have somebody in town to administer it, so he was going to tell the pastor the truth and ask him."

A logical explanation for Trevor's appointment with the pastor. At some point Nathan had said that there might be one, and she hadn't believed him.

I'm sorry, Trevor. Sorry I didn't have more faith in you. And even sorrier that you couldn't trust me.

"He was going down to the county seat to talk with some attorney he knew to handle it, but he had the accident." Rhoda's voice broke in a sob. "He never got to talk to the minister, and we never signed the papers."

Susannah pressed her fingers to her temples. Somehow she had to hold on long enough to do what had to be done.

Seeming to read her thoughts, Nathan put his hand over hers. She clung tightly, absorbing his strength.

"Rhoda, listen to me." She forced some assurance into her voice. "This is going to be all right. I'll take care of the trust."

The woman put a hand across her mouth, as if to hold back her sobs. She looked at Susannah with hope dawning in her eyes. "Do you mean that?"

"I'll take care of it. I don't know exactly how it will work, but I'll try and do just what Trevor would have done. He was right. Your child has to be provided for."

"That's all I want. Just for Thomas to be taken care of."

Susannah didn't doubt that. If Rhoda had wanted something for herself, she could have approached the family a long time ago. She'd had the perfect thing to hold over them, and she hadn't taken advantage of it.

"There's just one thing I want you to promise me." In the midst of her whirling thoughts, she knew this was important. "Enid Laine can never know about this. She couldn't handle it, and I don't want her to be hurt."

Rhoda drew a shuddering breath, and then nodded. "That's what Trevor said, too. I understand. She doesn't ever have to know about us."

There wasn't anything else to say. Or if there was, she couldn't find the words or the strength to say it.

She seemed to be floating far above herself. She looked down at Nathan's strong hand clasping hers as Rhoda thanked her and hurried out.

Over. It was over. Now she had to figure out how to live with the results.

Chapter Twelve

Nathan followed Rhoda to the kitchen door and closed it behind her. Not that he wanted to be rid of the poor woman, but he suspected Susannah had had all she could handle for the moment.

He walked back to her slowly, studying the tension in the line of her cheek and jaw. She looked brittle enough to break into a thousand pieces at a touch.

She was shocked, that was all. As soon as she'd adjusted to this new knowledge, she'd be relieved and thankful. Trevor hadn't betrayed her.

The betrayer had been Franklin. Nathan discovered that he wasn't really surprised by that fact.

He sat down next to Susannah at the table, taking both her hands in a firm grip. They were icy, and he tried to warm them between his palms. Somehow he had to find a way to ease her through the shock.

"It seems odd, after all this time, to know who Thomas's father really was. Rhoda did quite a job of keeping her secret."

She nodded, the movement seeming automatic. That unfocused stare of hers was unnerving. All he could think to do was to keep talking.

"Rhoda left Lakemont at the end of that last summer Trevor's family stayed at the summerhouse. She said she was going to the city to get a better job. Her folks had died, and there wasn't anything to keep her here. When she came back a couple of years later with a small child—"

He shrugged, trying to figure out what Susannah was thinking. She should be relieved, shouldn't she? All he could do was push on.

"I guess, by that time, people just accepted what she said, that she'd been married, but the marriage broke up after Thomas's birth."

Susannah finally managed to focus on him, her eyes losing some of that stunned appearance. "No one questioned Thomas's parentage?"

"Not that I know of. Apparently that was one the gossips missed." He felt a wave of relief. At least she was talking again. "Once Rhoda told us the truth, I found I wasn't too shocked about Franklin's behavior."

Susannah rubbed her forehead with an unsteady hand. "Why not? Did Franklin actually have that sort of reputation around here?"

"No. If that had been the case, people probably

would have guessed a long time ago that he was Thomas's father.''

''Then why?''

He tried to analyze a reaction that had been instinctive. ''Laine just had that kind of an extreme ego. His attitude seemed to say that the ordinary rules didn't apply to someone as successful as he was.''

''He always was larger than life, wasn't he? Always the center of everyone's attention.'' She was concentrating now, her hands warming to his touch.

His relief was palpable. She would be all right. ''How did you get along with him?''

She shrugged. ''I was always completely intimidated by him, to tell the truth. And Enid—well, Enid thought the sun rose and set on him.''

''You want to protect her from this.'' He could understand that. Why hurt the woman with this secret?

''I *have* to keep this from her. I don't know how she would cope with this news. She thought they had a perfect marriage.''

She seemed needlessly alarmed by the possibility.

''Enid doesn't have to know. It's all right. No one here will tell her.'' He stroked her hand, trying to calm her. ''And at least you know now that Trevor wasn't unfaithful to you. You must be relieved.''

''Relieved?'' She repeated the word as if she didn't know its meaning.

''Yes, relieved.'' His frustration mounted. Why

was she acting this way? "Of course it's upsetting about Franklin, but Trevor didn't betray you."

She seemed to sense his frustration. She took a deep breath, straightening, as if ready to take her burdens back on herself again.

"You have it wrong."

He frowned. "I have what wrong?"

"I didn't come to find out if Trevor was having an affair. I came to find out why he lied to me."

"Well, now you know. He—"

He stopped. How did that sentence finish?

"Exactly." Susannah's eyes darkened with pain. "The question is still there. He should have told me about Rhoda and Thomas."

"He probably intended to, once things were settled." He was bumbling around, hurting her through not knowing what to say or do.

"He didn't. My husband actually found it easier to lie to me than tell me the truth." Her voice broke.

"Susannah, the fact that he lied about this one thing doesn't mean you didn't know him."

How would he have felt if he'd learned that Linda had deceived him? He couldn't even imagine.

She pushed his rationale away with a single poignant gesture. "It means he didn't trust me with something basic and fundamental. That says something pretty devastating about our marriage, doesn't it?"

He wanted to comfort her. He didn't know how.

There wasn't anything he could say that would make this better.

And unfortunately he remembered what had happened the last time he'd tried to comfort her. Things had gotten totally out of control between them. Maybe he'd better be content to hold her hand.

"Nobody can look inside someone else's marriage," he said carefully.

"No." The single word seemed heavily laden with sorrow and regret.

"I wish I could make it better."

She managed a smile. "You have. Thank you for being here. For holding my hand." She let go suddenly, as if having called attention to it, she knew it was a mistake.

"You asked me to help you. That's all I've tried to do. I'm sorry it didn't turn out better for you." Sorrier than she was ever going to know.

"I think I've leaned on you long enough." She straightened, as if determined to take her burdens back on her own shoulders. "It's time I went back home and got on with things."

He discovered he didn't want to think about her leaving. But he'd have to.

"You won't leave Lakemont before the homecoming parade, will you? If given a choice, I know Jen would much rather have you there than me."

Susannah blinked, as if coming back from a far distance to the world of homecoming parades and fifteen-year-olds. "No, I can't miss that. I promised her I'd be there. But then on Saturday I'll leave."

He heard what she didn't say. Once she left Lakemont, she wouldn't be back. She wouldn't want to return to the site of so much pain.

She was leaving, and he certainly didn't want to ask her to stay. So why did the thought make him feel as if his heart was being wrenched out of place?

"Careful now." Daniel took Susannah's arm as they crossed the street in the wake of the parade. "You don't want to trip on anything."

"I'm fine." Susannah realized it was the same thing she was constantly saying to Nathan. "You know, your son must get that protective streak of his from you."

"Maybe so." Daniel took the step up to the sidewalk easily for someone Nathan insisted had to be cosseted. "Nathan always has wanted to take care of people."

"I suppose that's why he went into police work." It made sense, for a person who needed to protect.

"I guess so. It was something he wanted to do from the time he was a little kid. I'd have to say he's a bit too protective of me at times." He glanced at her face. "Maybe you feel as if he's that way with you, too."

She nodded. "I do, but I suppose that's natural enough, given what he's been through."

He was protective because she was pregnant, as Linda had been, not because he cared about her.

That thought hurt more than it should. How long was it going to take her to get over Nathan? It wasn't as if they'd ever had a real relationship. That should make it easier to forget and move on.

Somehow she didn't think it would. Nathan had found a place in her heart. Even the baby might not be able to crowd him out entirely.

She and Daniel joined the crowd moving slowly toward the park that ran along the lakeshore. The small parade that had started at the high school had ended there, and one of the local service clubs was running a barbecue to raise money for charity. Already she could smell the aromas of sizzling meat and pungent sauce.

"Nathan tells me you're planning to leave us tomorrow." Daniel didn't look as if the news gave him any pleasure.

"I'm afraid so." How much had Nathan told him? Not everything, she was sure. "I've done what I can here, and I'm feeling better about things. It's time to get on with having this baby."

"We'll miss you." He clasped her elbow as a cluster of kids surged by them. "I know Philadelphia's your home, but you have to admit, Philly probably doesn't do a homecoming parade the way we do."

She smiled. "You're right about that." Homemade floats, one marching band and three fire trucks.

But it had been touching, all the same. "Jen looked as if she was having a good time."

Actually, Jen, with her face scrubbed free of makeup for her role as a flower on the float, had looked better than Susannah had ever seen her. And happier, too, leaning across the float to chatter to the other flowers and tossing candy to the kids who lined the street.

"I hope so." His face clouded a little. "I'd like— well, I'd like her to feel she belongs here, for however long she stays."

"You have a good heart, Daniel."

He shook his head, smiling a little. "Can't help caring about that girl, can I? Actually, I'd like you to feel you belong here, too."

Her heart seemed to clench. "That's a nice thought, but I'm afraid my life is elsewhere."

For a moment she couldn't even picture the life she'd intended to have. The thought sent a ripple of panic through her. What had happened to all her plans?

"You sure about that? Lakemont is a good place to raise a child."

"I imagine it is."

In that instant her imagination did take over, presenting her with a picture of her daughter skipping along these safe streets, riding on a float with everyone watching knowing who she was and caring about her.

The trouble was that her imagination was com-

pleting that picture with someone else—a strong
masculine figure who'd want to be a father to Sarah
and a husband to her. And she knew that was never
going to happen.

Nathan didn't want that. He'd made his feelings
clear. He didn't even think it was possible to put a
family together from people who weren't related.
Even if he were able to get past his feelings for
Linda and love her, he'd never be able to treat her
daughter as his own child.

So there could be nothing between them. If she
ever did marry again, it would have to be to someone who saw Sarah as a daughter, not as a deficit.

She heard a brief beep of a horn and turned to see
a car pulling to the curb next to them. No, not just
a car. A police cruiser, with Nathan at the wheel.
She'd seen him earlier, when he'd driven slowly
down the parade route in advance of the parade,
making sure everything was in readiness.

He'd been smiling then. He wasn't now. Something tightened inside her as Nathan got out of the
car and advanced toward them, his determined stride
seeming to sweep everyone and everything out of
his way.

He came to a halt in front of them, his frowning
gaze moving from her to Daniel. "I take it Jen
hasn't been with you."

Daniel shook his head. "I figured we'd meet up
at the barbecue."

"I told her to check in with me after the parade." Nathan's tone was accusing. "She didn't show."

His father didn't seem disturbed. "She probably had to change her clothes."

"She's had plenty of time to do that." Nathan looked around, frowning. "Where is she?"

"I'm sure she's around here somewhere." Susannah wanted to wipe that fierce look off his face, both for Jen's sake and his own. "Maybe she just forgot. Or maybe you missed her in the crowd."

He shook his head stubbornly. "It was the last thing I said to her when I dropped her off. And if she'd been where she was supposed to be, I couldn't have missed her."

Well, maybe he couldn't. Presumably a police officer looked at a crowd differently from the average person.

Daniel was scanning the crowd, too, apparently picking up on Nathan's concern. He nodded toward a group of teens who clustered around a popcorn stand.

"There's Marcy Peters, from the youth group. She was on the float. I'll go ask her if she knows where Jen is."

He moved away from them, working his way steadily through the crowd. He really didn't look as if he needed the cotton wool Nathan kept trying to wrap him in.

Not her business, she reminded herself, and turned back to Nathan, to meet his frowning gaze.

"Are you sure you should be out in this crowd?" he asked with an abrupt turn of subject. "You might get jostled."

"The baby is well protected."

"You aren't. You could lose your balance."

"I'm fine." For the hundredth time. His overprotectiveness might be understandable if he cared enough to want her to stay. "You're overreacting."

Someone bumped against her from behind, and his steadying arm shot around her instantly. "Maybe not."

"Yes, you are." She forced herself to step away from the protection of his strong grasp. "You're overreacting about me, and you're overreacting about Jen."

His face tightened. "It's not overreacting. She let me down, and I'm responsible for her."

"And I'm not, I know." She glared at him. "That doesn't mean I don't care about her."

Admit you care, Nathan. It won't hurt you.

Daniel came back before she could say anything else, and that was probably a good thing. Her emotions were definitely getting the better of her.

Pregnancy hormones, she told herself. Bubbling up and making her say things she shouldn't.

Daniel looked worried. "Marcy says Jen was changed and out of there over half an hour ago. She saw her leave the rest room, and Jen didn't head toward the barbecue."

"Did she see which way Jen went?" Nathan

snapped the question as coolly as if he were talking to a witness instead of his father.

"She saw her get into a pickup truck. A rusted-out red pickup."

Nathan's jaw looked tight enough to break. "Thad Ferguson."

His concern seemed to spread across the space between them, infecting her. She looked at him, and for an instant it was as if they were alone in the crowd.

"Are you sure?"

"I'm sure." His tone was grim. "She wasn't supposed to go anywhere, and certainly not for a ride in that death trap of a vehicle."

"I'll go and look for her." Daniel took a step before Nathan stopped him with a hand on his arm.

"No, Dad."

Daniel's stubborn look was remarkably like Nathan's. "Stop coddling me. I'm perfectly capable of driving a car around town to look for Jen."

"I'm sure you are." Nathan's voice had softened. "But someone should stay at the barbecue in case she shows up here. You stay here and watch for her, and I'll go see if I can find that pickup."

For a moment they frowned at each other, looking very alike. Then Daniel nodded.

Nathan turned toward the cruiser, but she managed to get there first. He sent her a harassed look.

"What are you doing?"

"I'm going with you."

"Don't be ridiculous. You go back and wait with my father."

She gave him glare for glare. "I'm going with you," she repeated. She yanked at the door, which refused to open. Stubborn, just like Nathan. "So let's stop wasting time and start looking."

Apparently he realized further argument was useless. He reached around her to open the door without a word, then circled the vehicle and slid behind the wheel.

Nathan closed the door with a thud, abruptly cutting off the noise of the crowd and the music that had been blaring from somewhere. They were alone together, and that knowledge seemed to dance along her skin. Being alone with Nathan wasn't a good idea.

Jen, she reminded herself. This was about Jen, not about her feelings for Nathan.

He started the car and drove slowly along a block crowded with people heading for the barbecue. She automatically searched one side of the street, knowing he was doing the same on the opposite side.

They'd reached the end of the block when she knew she had to break the silence.

"She's not going to thank you for tracking her down," she said finally.

"Don't you think I know that?" His jaw was clenched tight. "Believe me, if I thought she'd forgotten to check in because she was out with a bunch of kids, I wouldn't be worried. I might be irritated, but not worried. But this wasn't just forgetting. She planned this.''

Obviously she had. A quiver of concern went through Susannah. What had Jen gotten herself into?

''This kid Thad—she said something about him the other day. That he'd been nice to her.'' She remembered the rest of it. ''That if she had a boyfriend, maybe the other kids would feel like she belonged.''

She probably could have given Jen some better advice, if only she'd thought about it more carefully.

''Did you know she was going off with him today?''

''Of course not.'' Did Nathan think she was a complete idiot?

''Sorry.'' He shot her an apologetic look. ''I know you wouldn't encourage her to do something stupid. I've looked for straying kids before, but not one—''

He stopped, but she could finish the sentence for him.

''Not one you care about.''

''Yes.'' He gripped the wheel as if he intended to wrench it off.

At least he'd admitted it.

''I'm sorry for what I said earlier—I mean, if it sounded as if I thought you didn't care. I know you do.''

His smile flickered. ''You knew I cared about Jennifer before I did, as a matter of fact. I thought she was just a nuisance. But right now I'd give a lot to have that nuisance safe at home.''

Or safely back in her mother's erratic custody? Nathan had expressed the caring she knew he felt for the girl, but that didn't mean he'd changed his attitude.

Unreasonable tears clogged her throat. How happy would he be when she and Jen were both gone?

Chapter Thirteen

His life would be better when Susannah and Jennifer were both out of it. If Nathan told himself that often enough, maybe he'd start to believe it.

He shot a sideways glance at Susannah. They'd been driving around for nearly an hour. She looked tired, and she was probably hungry.

She also looked beautiful, so beautiful that it seemed to kick him right in the heart. Who was he kidding, thinking things would be better when Susannah was gone? Life might go back to normal, but it sure wouldn't be better.

He had to try to convince her to take it easy. The stress of riding around looking for a missing teenager couldn't be good for her.

"Look, we don't seem to be getting very far. Why don't I take you home, or at least back to the barbecue? You probably ought to get something to eat.''

Susannah shook her head. ''I'm not hungry. Maybe you should check with your father again.''

Dad would have called if Jen had turned up, but he picked up the phone anyway. Any action seemed preferable to driving up and down the grid of narrow streets, looking for the telltale signs of a teen party, wondering where Jen was and how she was handling herself.

What if she wasn't at a party? What if she'd decided to run away, and talked that kid into helping her? How long should he wait before making this search official?

His father picked up on the first ring. ''Did you find her?''

''Not yet. Don't worry, we will.''

''I know you will, son. I know.''

He hung up, shaking his head at Susannah, even though he was sure she'd figured out that terse exchange. He gestured toward the police radio. ''I could make this official, you know. But if I do, there's no going back. In the absence of her mother, Jen could be put into foster care.''

''I know. That's what I've been worrying about.'' She shook her head. ''We have to find her.''

They were both professionals at this. They both knew what could happen to Jennifer.

''So far she's doing a pretty good job of keeping

out of sight.'' His jaw clenched tightly. *Where are you, Jen? What's going on in that head of yours?*

Susannah leaned forward, pressing her hands against the dashboard as if to make the car go faster. *This isn't good for her,* he thought again, but knew he couldn't say anything that would make her go back.

''Isn't there anyplace else kids hang out? Where did you go when you had the car and were out with a girl you wanted to impress?''

The only girl he'd ever wanted to impress was Linda, but it wouldn't help to think about that now.

''The quarry.'' He hit the brake. ''The quarry has always been a favorite parking spot. I don't know why I didn't think of it sooner.''

He took a quick look and then made a U-turn, his mind reaching ahead toward the road that led up to the ridge and the local version of a lovers' lane. He'd been obsessing about having to break up an illicit party, but Susannah was right. This was just as likely and just as unpleasant. Jen was up there alone with Thad.

''How far is it?'' Concern laced Susannah's voice.

''Four or five miles.'' He glanced at her again, feeling as if there was something he should be saying to her, something left unsaid in their past few conversations. ''I guess I didn't act like it, but I appreciate your coming along. I know you care about Jen.''

"She's a nice kid. She's certainly been good to me." She smiled. "All those trays she carried up. That was above and beyond the call of duty."

"She likes you." Why wouldn't she? Susannah had been far more understanding than he had.

A sense of failure rode him. He hadn't wanted Jen complicating their lives, and he'd probably made that only too clear to her. If something happened to her, it would be his fault.

"Don't beat yourself up." Susannah reached out to touch his arm, and he seemed to feel a flood of sympathy down to his bones. "She knows you care about her, even when she's fighting you every step of the way."

He frowned out at shadows reaching across the road ahead as the sun dipped low over the mountain.

"Relating to teenage girls isn't my strong suit. I never know what to say to her."

"Just listen to her. Support her." Her voice grew softer. "The way you've done for me. I don't think I've told you how much I appreciate everything you've done. I couldn't have gotten through this without you."

This conversation was starting to sound like goodbye. Something hard and lonely gripped his heart.

"Look." Susannah's voice rose with a note of relief. "There she is."

He didn't know what was stronger, anger or gratitude, when he saw Jen walking along the side of the road. Walking.

Suddenly the anger predominated, but it wasn't for her. What had happened with Thad, that she was walking?

He pulled to a stop and was out in a second. Jen turned her face away from him, but not before he saw her tears. She'd been so happy riding on that float, and now her shoulders were hunched, her face tearstained. His heart seemed wrenched from its place, and every other emotion melted in the need to comfort her.

"Hey, it's all right." He reached for her, one part of his mind telling him that she wouldn't welcome comfort from him. "Are you okay?"

"Fine." Some defiance clung to her voice, but she avoided his eyes.

He heard Susannah getting out of the car behind him and felt her willing him to take it easy. Susannah might know better than he did how to handle a teenage girl, but this was his job.

He kept his concentration on Jen. If he didn't say the right thing this time, the girl would never let him get this close again.

"Sure you're fine," he said gently. "But you're crying, and I'd like to help."

She flung her head up, misery in her eyes. "You ought to be happy. You told me Thad was a jerk, and you were right, just like you are about everything."

"Not about everything." He touched her arm lightly. "I didn't give you enough credit for taking care of yourself. Here you are walking home instead of sitting up at the quarry with Thad.''

A little bravado crossed her face. ''Yeah, well, who did he think he was kidding, acting like he cared about me? He doesn't care about anybody but himself.''

If he caught that kid doing anything, including jaywalking, he was going to throw the book at him.

''I'm sorry, Jen.'' Carefully, carefully. ''For your sake, I wish I'd been wrong about him.'' He reached his arm out to her, wondering if he dared give her a hug.

''Yeah. Me, too.''

There was a little quaver in her voice. She held herself erect an instant longer, and then she took a step that dissolved the space between them. She leaned against him. He hugged her close, his throat tight.

She buried her face in his jacket. ''Thanks for not saying you told me so.''

''I'll remind you of that some other time. For now, let's forget about Thad Ferguson.''

She sniffed a little. ''I can't.'' Her voice was filled with misery. ''He'll go tell everyone his version of what happened, and they'll all be laughing at me.''

''Not if you beat him to it,'' Susannah said. ''Go back to the barbecue with us now. Put a smile on your face and act like you're having a great time.''

Jen drew back enough to look at her. ''You think?'' A little hope dawned in her eyes.

"I think most people treat you the way you let them think you should be treated. And if they don't—well, that's their problem, not yours."

He'd have suggested going home, but Susannah was right. The sooner Jen got out there with the other kids, the better off she'd be.

Jen hesitated a moment longer. Then she seemed to screw up her courage. "Okay. Let's do it. I'm not gonna let him mess up my homecoming."

"You've got it, ladies." He opened the car doors for them. "It'll be my pleasure to treat you both to a barbecue and all the dessert you can eat."

Thank You, Lord. He didn't say it often enough, but he felt it now. *Thank You.*

They got in and he slid behind the wheel, picking up the phone. He'd better let Dad know Jen was all right. And that they were coming to join him for the barbecue, for all the world as if they were a family.

Nathan let his father and Jen out at the front of the lodge a couple of hours later, then turned toward Susannah, sitting across from him in the front seat of the car. The parking-lot lights illuminated her face, picking out the delicate line of her cheek and the shadows under her eyes.

She looked tired, too tired. This night had been too much for her. He should have overridden her objections and brought her home long ago.

Should have, maybe. Not that she'd have agreed to it, no matter what he said.

"You really ought to stay at the lodge again tonight." He had to give this a try. "You don't want to be at the cottage alone."

"I'll be fine."

He lifted an eyebrow at the familiar refrain. "Seems to me I've heard that before."

"Well, I will." Defensiveness threaded her voice. "I really need to get my things organized in order to leave tomorrow. It'll be easier to do that if I just spend the night there."

What she said made sense, but he still didn't like it. Not that it was his business either to like or dislike what she chose to do. He put the car in gear and drove down the lane toward the cottage.

She was leaving. When they said goodbye tonight it would be just that, goodbye. He had to be off to the county seat early in the morning for a hearing, and by the time he returned, Susannah would undoubtedly be gone.

He couldn't kid himself that they'd see each other again. She'd never want to come to Lakemont again. It had been the scene of too much grief.

She was leaving. That was what he'd wanted from the moment he'd encountered her. Then his attitude had been perfectly straightforward. Now...

Now he was trapped in a morass of feelings he couldn't begin to sort out. Only one thing was perfectly clear. He didn't want Susannah to walk out of his life.

He glanced at her as his headlights touched the

cottage porch. She stared out the window, as withdrawn and far away as if she'd already left.

That was best, wasn't it? He'd always known God had given him the love of a lifetime in Linda. He and Linda had been destined for each other. So how could he possibly have feelings for Susannah?

He couldn't. Unfortunately his heart didn't seem to be listening. Linda had been comfort and familiarity. Susannah was strong, complex and vulnerable all at once. He shouldn't care. But he did.

He turned off the ignition, got out of the car and went around to open the door for her. Neither of them spoke, and he felt as if they were both moving in slow motion as he helped her out of the car.

"Thank you." She waited while he closed the door, then put her hand on his arm to walk up the steps.

It was a simple enough gesture, but it made his heart clench. Susannah had grown to rely on him. Almost without his noticing that it was happening, she'd grabbed a piece of his life and become an important part of it. How were they going to get along without each other?

She wobbled on the steps, as if the baby's increasing weight was almost more than she could carry. He steadied her, a wave of tenderness sweeping over him. He wanted to brush every obstacle from her path. He wanted to guarantee her happiness. But no one could do that.

"Thank you." Her voice was soft, almost breathless. Because of the weight of the pregnancy, no doubt. Not because he was near.

"You should have stayed at the lodge."

"All my things are here. I have to get packed. Besides, I like it here."

She unlocked the door, swinging it open so that the room inside seemed to reach out to them. She'd left a lamp on in the living room while she was out, and its light brought the warm colors of the room to life.

Out here there was only cool night air and the pale yellow glow of the porch light, imitating the pale glow of the full moon.

Susannah looked up at him, eyes serious, as if she sensed his inner turmoil.

"Would you like to come in?"

He wanted to. He wanted to walk into that warm, lighted room with Susannah. He wanted to take her in his arms and ask her to stay.

"Better not. It's late, and I know you have a lot of packing to do."

Something shadowed her eyes, and she nodded. "Well. I guess this is goodbye, then."

"I guess so."

Don't go.

He couldn't say that. He couldn't offer her his heart, and what other reason could there be for her to stay?

"I can't leave without thanking you again."

"You don't—"

She held up her hand to silence his protest. "I know, you don't want to hear it, but you've really been a rock." Her eyes shimmered, as if they were filling with the tears she was determined not to shed. "No one could have blamed you for keeping your distance under the circumstances. I'll never forget how you stood by me."

He didn't deserve her gratitude. "I didn't do much. You came here to find out the truth, and you'd have done it with or without me. I'm just sorry the whole thing has caused you so much pain."

Sorry I've caused you pain.

That was the reality, wasn't it? They had feelings for each other, and he was backing away. Keeping his distance, as she'd said.

"Sometimes the pain is worth it." Her voice was very soft. A tear escaped to trickle down her cheek.

He couldn't ignore the impulse to reach up, touch her cheek, blot the tear with his finger. They were close, so close. All he had to do was move slightly, and they'd be kissing.

No. He couldn't. He couldn't give her his heart. He wasn't sure he had one left to give.

He let his hand drop and saw the light die from her eyes.

"Good night, Susannah."

Goodbye.

He turned away.

*   *   *

She was nearly ready. In an hour she'd be gone. Susannah sank into Linda's rocking chair the next morning, her Bible in her hands, and looked out at the sunlight sparkling on the lake.

The first time she'd looked at the scene, the trees across the lake had been barely touched with color. Now they were at their peak, as if this was one last vibrant trumpet call of life before their winter sleep.

She leaned back, stroking her hand down over her stomach. She knew now why this rocker felt as if it had been placed here for this purpose. Because it had. Linda had sat here, looking out over the lake, dreaming of her life with Nathan once their baby had come.

Linda hadn't lived to see her dreams come true. As for Susannah's own dreams—well, they'd changed out of all recognition.

She barely seemed to know the woman she'd been when she and Trevor had gotten married. That woman had been so foolish, thinking she knew what love meant, trying to build a real marriage on a faulty foundation and convince herself it was love.

Love. Her heart ached with it. She knew now what kind of love it took to build a marriage. But that love just wasn't meant to be.

Goodbye.

Her future lay clearly ahead of her, even if it wasn't the one she'd anticipated. She'd go back to Philadelphia and make the final arrangements for her baby's birth.

Once Sarah had come, she'd be busy learning how to be a mother. Sarah and Enid would be the only family she had. Maybe it wasn't a storybook ending, but she'd have a satisfying, useful life.

She'd see to it that Rhoda and her son were provided for. That would be her only remaining link to Lakemont and all that had happened here.

She levered herself out of the rocking chair and put the Bible down on the table. Now, the next thing—

The contraction that hit her was powerful enough to knock everything else out of her mind. She caught her breath and gripped the lamp table, hanging on until the contraction subsided.

This couldn't be labor. It was too early for that. Maybe the pain had been one of those practice contractions the doctor had warned her about. Cautiously she made her way to the bedroom, alert for any changes in her body.

Moving slowly, she put the last few things into her suitcase. She'd call Jen, who would come and help her load the car. They'd say their goodbyes. When she got back to Philadelphia she could call her doctor's office and report how she felt, just to be on the safe side.

She was fine. She'd said those words to Nathan so many times that it had become a joke between them.

If he were here now, he'd want to rush her to the

hospital, which was foolish. Her due date was nearly four weeks away.

She snapped the suitcase shut. So it was a good thing Nathan wasn't here. And she wouldn't let herself dwell on those moments the night before when they'd stood so close and she'd thought he was going to ask her to stay.

Forget it. Call Jen and—

The pain hit again. This time she recognized it for what it was.

You'll know when it's the real thing, people said, and they were right. The contraction built and built, and she clutched the bed, trying to remember how to breathe.

When it finally eased off, she looked at her watch. Why hadn't she timed the contractions? She wasn't sure how long the pain had lasted, but she did know they'd been close. Too close.

Panic swept over her in a suffocating wave. The baby was coming.

Help us, Father. Keep Sarah safe. Help me know what to do.

She grabbed the phone, fingers fumbling as she punched in the lodge number. Nathan. She wanted Nathan.

But it was Daniel who answered the phone.

Careful. Don't alarm him. All of Nathan's concerns for Daniel's health raced through her mind.

"Is Nathan there?" She tried to keep the panic

from her voice. The hands of her watch moved inexorably toward the next contraction.

"I'm sorry, Susannah, but he had that hearing over at the county seat this morning. He's already left. If you're ready to load the car, Jen and I will come over."

"No, it's not that."

What was the best move? Could she call for a taxi, or didn't Lakemont have such things? The next contraction started, and she fought down a gasp.

"Susannah, what is it?" Daniel's voice sharpened. "What's wrong?"

All her good resolutions vanished. She had to have help. "I—I'm in labor."

"We'll be right there."

Before she could protest and tell him to call an ambulance instead, he'd hung up. And by the time she'd ridden out the contraction and made her way to the living room, a car was pulling up outside. Daniel and Jen erupted from either side of it, racing toward the door.

"Are you all right?" Jen reached her first, putting an arm around her.

"Of course she is. She's just having a baby." Daniel reached her other side. "How close are they?"

"Too close." She searched his face for strain, but found only strength and comfort. "You shouldn't have come. If you'll just call for an ambulance—"

"Nonsense. We can have you to the hospital in half the time. Is there a bag you want to take?"

"I just packed all my things." She felt absurdly like crying. "I'm not ready yet. I was going to pack a hospital bag after I got back to Philadelphia."

He patted her hand. Like Nathan, he was a rock. "It's okay. Let's get you to the hospital first, then we'll pick up anything you need and bring it to you." He glanced across her at Jen. "Ready?"

The girl nodded, her thin face determined, and tightened the grasp she had on Susannah. "Let's go."

They made it to the bottom of the steps before another contraction halted their little caravan. Daniel talked reassuringly throughout the pain, while Jen rubbed her shoulders.

"They're too close," she said when she could speak again. "It's too early." She shouldn't let the fear into her voice, but she couldn't help it.

"Babies come when they want to, regardless of the calendar," Daniel said practically. He helped her into the back seat, and Jen slid in with her. "Don't you worry. Jenny, you hold on to her. We're going to have a baby."

Nathan. She should be ashamed of herself for the need she felt to say his name. *I wish you were here.*

Chapter Fourteen

Nathan walked out of the county courthouse with a sense of relief. Given Judge Cranwell's temper, hearings in front of him were always tricky, but this one had gone well. He strode toward his car, switching on the cell phone that he'd had to turn off in the courtroom.

By the time he reached the car, the phone rang.

"Sloane," he said.

"We had to take Susannah to the hospital." Jen's voice, high-pitched with excitement or fear, poured into his ear, setting his heart pounding. "Your father says you should come right away."

He was already starting the car, dread filling his mind, nearly blanking out his ability to think. "What's wrong? Is she all right?"

"I don't know. Nobody's telling us anything. Daniel went back to talk to the nurse again." Jen's voice trembled on the verge of tears. "Please come, Nathan. We need you."

"I'll be there as fast as I can." He tried to sound confident through the fear that had him by the throat. "Just hang on. I'll be there."

He took a quick glance behind him and then whipped out of the parking space. He'd turn on the siren as soon as he reached the highway. It wouldn't take long to get back to Lakemont. He'd be there in time.

You weren't before, a voice whispered in his heart. *Linda and the baby died because you weren't there.*

This was different. He had to believe that. This was different. They'd already taken Susannah to the hospital. She was in good hands.

It was too soon. The baby wasn't due for weeks, from what Susannah had told him. If she was in labor, what did that mean for her and for the baby?

Please. He couldn't seem to form a coherent prayer. *Please. She has to be all right. I can't lose her.*

You were going to lose her anyway. You were letting her go away without telling her how you feel.

I don't know how I feel.

But that was a lie, and he knew it. He loved her. He couldn't lose her.

Half an hour later he strode out of the elevator on the obstetrics floor, heart still pounding. The waiting room was opposite the elevator, and the first person he saw was his father, then Jen.

They were smiling.

Smiling. The iron fist that had been gripping his heart relaxed.

"Susannah? Is she okay?"

"She's fine. Just fine." He couldn't remember the last time he'd seen his father grin that way. "We got her here in time."

"We did it," Jen crowed, grabbing his arm.

She didn't look like the same girl, with her face innocent of makeup and her eyes sparkling like stars. She couldn't seem to stop smiling.

"I sat in back with her all the way and helped her." Her words stumbled over each other in excitement. "She said I really helped. Said she didn't know how she'd have made it without me."

"Hey, I helped, too." Daniel nudged her, grinning. "Don't I get some credit for driving her here?"

"You shouldn't have driven—" he began, then realized it was fruitless. No matter what he said, his father had already driven. He'd gotten Susannah to the hospital in time.

"Don't you want to know about the baby?" Jen shook his arm. "Don't you?"

He felt the familiar tension in the pit of his stomach. "What about the baby?"

"A six-pound girl. Sarah Grace." Daniel pounded his shoulder as if he were the father. "She's little, but she's perfectly healthy. Susannah thinks maybe they miscalculated her due date, because little Sarah sure doesn't look like a preemie.''

"She has the prettiest blue eyes and just a little bit of dark hair, but Susannah says that's how hers was and it will probably turn red.'' Jen seemed equally confident. "I got to see her when she was only fifteen minutes old. Susannah says I can hold her later.''

"Me first,'' his father said.

"Susannah says…''

Nathan shook his head. The two of them were squabbling over the baby like—

Like a father and daughter.

Jen didn't carry any of Daniel's blood in her veins, but that couldn't negate the bond between them. Blood ties or not, Jen had become a part of Daniel's family. He was going to find it hard to part with her when the time came.

And how did he feel about that?

"Susannah wants to see you,'' Daniel said. "Room 412. The patient rooms are right down that hall.''

"I know.''

He did. He had taken the tour with Linda, and things apparently hadn't changed since then.

"Are you okay?'' That might have been pity in his father's eyes.

"Of course.'' He straightened his shoulders. "I'll go right now.''

He started down the hall, trying not to let memories seep in. To his surprise, that time seemed very long ago.

Now was Susannah, and her baby. He discovered a lump in his throat and tried to swallow it. What was he going to say to Susannah? She'd needed help, and he hadn't been there.

He reached the door. Stared for a moment at the number. Then he rapped.

"Come in." Susannah's voice sounded perfectly normal, as if she hadn't just had a baby.

He pushed open the door, bracing himself for a flood of feelings.

Sunlight poured through the opened blind on the window across the small room from him. It touched Susannah's face, turned toward him. She was propped up in the hospital bed, her hair curling damply around her face. She looked radiant. Beautiful.

For a moment he couldn't speak at all. He could only look at her. Finally he found his voice.

"How are you?"

"I'm fine. I'm wonderful." Her eyes shone like stars. She held out her hand to him as if his being here was the most natural thing in the world.

He approached cautiously, clumsily, feeling like the proverbial bull in a china shop. The tiny room was crowded with things, most of which he didn't want to look at too closely, including a metal-and-acrylic bassinet that contained a pink-blanket-wrapped bundle.

He averted his eyes and concentrated on Susannah. That wasn't hard to do, not when he'd spent the past hour fearing he'd lost her.

You'd already lost her, that voice in his brain reminded him. *You'd already lost her, because you were willing to let her go.*

"I'm sorry." He was close enough to take her hand, and he held it carefully, half-afraid to touch her. "I wasn't there to help you."

Her eyes darkened, as if she heard all the sorrow in those words that he couldn't express.

"I was fine." As soon as she said the familiar words, she smiled, as if hearing the echo of all the times she'd said them. "Your father and Jen were terrific. Terrific."

"So they tell me. I thought the next thing they'd say was that they delivered the baby themselves."

How could he be standing here talking so politely about his father and Jen as if they were the only ones who crowded his heart?

"No, we got here in time for the doctor to do that. I really am all right, you know."

"Thank God." The words were a heartfelt prayer.

"Yes," she said softly. "I have been." She looked at him, as if weighing something in her mind. "Don't you want to see my daughter?"

"Of course," he lied.

He forced himself to walk to the bassinet, tried to

look without seeing at the baby who could only remind him of the child he'd lost. He concentrated on the pink blanket instead of the baby who slept in it.

"She's beautiful." He swung back to Susannah. "Like her mother."

"Thanks." Tears swam in her eyes. She pushed a hand through her hair. "But I look a wreck."

"You look beautiful." He reached her side again, turning his back on the bassinet. He took her hand in his, carefully avoiding the bruise where they'd probably put an intravenous in. "I'm so glad you're all right. When I finally got the call, I thought—"

He stopped. He would not compare Susannah with Linda. He would think only of her, of the feelings he had for her. He wouldn't deny what was in his heart any longer.

"I'm sorry I scared everyone…" she began.

"Scared, yes. But fearing I was going to lose you made me face the truth." He lifted her hand to his cheek, praying she could see into his heart and believe what he was saying. "And the truth is I love you, Susannah. I love you."

Susannah could only stare at him, knowing her eyes must be wide with shock. She didn't seem to be breathing, but her heart was beating so loudly Nathan must be able to hear it.

He pressed his cheek against her palm. His skin was warm and rough, sending a shaft of pure pleasure from her palm straight to her heart. She seemed to be floating several inches above the smooth firm surface of the hospital bed.

She found her voice, though she could hardly hear herself above the singing of her heart. "Would you mind saying that again?"

Nathan's devastating smile warmed his face, chasing away the lines of strain. He turned his head slightly, so that his lips were against her palm.

"I love you, Susannah. Please say you have feelings for me."

Her smile trembled on the verge of tears. "I love you." She took a breath, hardly able to believe this moment had come. "I can't believe I can finally say it."

He bent over her, pressing his cheek carefully against hers, and she knew this was real, and not some childbirth-induced fantasy.

"I'm afraid to touch you." His voice shook a little. "Are you sure you're all right?"

"Never better." She slipped her arms around his broad shoulders, drawing him closer.

"I love you," he said again, a note of wonder in his tone. He drew back a little. "You'll stay here, won't you? You won't go away."

She met his gaze seriously. "This is happening pretty fast. Are you sure that's what you want?"

"More than anything. I know we can make a success of this. I know we can."

Oddly, something about his very insistence concerned her. Then she knew what bothered her. He hadn't mentioned her daughter.

Don't overreact, she told herself.

Sarah Grace probably didn't even seem real to him yet. Just because she was totally wrapped up in the wonderment of that new little life, she could hardly expect him to feel the same. Still…

"I have the baby to consider." She said the words carefully.

"The baby," he repeated, something wary lurking in the depths of his eyes.

The first cold trickle of reality snaked across her skin, making her shiver.

She pushed herself up cautiously in the bed, trying for a rationality she didn't feel. "We have to talk about this. How are you going to feel about the baby?"

His fingers tightened on hers, but she didn't think he even realized it. She could feel the tension that went through him, and she saw again his face that night at the church supper when Jen had thrust a baby toward him.

He never willingly touches a baby. That was what Daniel had said.

Nathan straightened, seeming to fill the tiny room. "I love you, Susannah. Naturally I'll take on responsibility for your child."

Her heart was suddenly a lead weight in her chest. Responsibility.

"Nathan, you feel responsibility for everyone

around you." He felt responsible for Jen, but he still wanted to be rid of her. "This will take more than that."

His face tightened. "Since I lost my son—" He stopped, mouth clamping shut as if the words were too painful.

"I know." His pain seemed to touch her very soul. "I'm sorry. But I have to know how you're going to relate to my baby. You see that, don't you?"

"I haven't been able to get close to a baby without feeling like my heart is ripping open." His face twisted. "Is that what you want to know?"

"Nathan—"

"All I can say is that I'll try. I'll try to care for her the way you want."

The way she wanted. Her heart seemed to crumble slowly into pieces, one after another falling away into black nothingness. He wasn't going to be able to love her daughter. He might want to, for her sake, but he couldn't.

"This isn't going to work, is it?" She whispered the words.

Something that almost looked like anger flared in his eyes, and he gripped her hands fiercely. "It will work. We'll make it work."

She shook her head, the cold reaching her soul. "No." That was the hardest word. "It won't."

Nathan was staring at her in pain and shock. She had to find the words that would explain what she felt, even though explanations couldn't make this better.

"I know what mistake Trevor and I made in our marriage," she said carefully. "We settled for too little from each other."

"I'm not Trevor."

Please, Father. I see this so clearly now. Help me find the way to tell him.

"I made a mistake then that I won't repeat." Carefully she drew her hands away from his. It was better not to be touching when she said this. "I believe I have it in me to give and to receive true devotion. I can't settle for less than that from you. We'd just end up hurting each other."

Nathan's face was a rigid mask. "I'm willing to risk that."

"I'm sorry, Nathan." She had to force the words out through a choked throat. "I have a child to consider. I'm not willing to take the risk. If you can't give us your whole heart, I'd rather have nothing."

He stared at her for a long moment, his eyes dark with pain.

The pink blanket stirred. Sarah Grace began to whimper softly. The sound escalated until it seemed to fill the hospital room.

Everything about Nathan tightened in response to that small sound, as if it took all his will to keep from running away.

"You see," she whispered. There was a gaping hole where her heart had been.

"I'm sorry." He uttered the words through set lips. Then he turned and walked out of her life.

Two days had passed, and Nathan was no closer to regaining his equilibrium than he had been the moment he walked out of Susannah's hospital room. He drove along the lake road toward the lodge, more slowly than usual for him.

Anyone looking at him could see nothing out of the ordinary. Of course not. It was only inside that he felt as if his world had been knocked off its axis. It would probably never be right again.

His tension kicked up a notch when the lodge sign came into view. He wasn't used to feeling that way about his home, but he couldn't help it.

He understood why his father had insisted Susannah come back to the lodge to recuperate for a few days before returning to Philadelphia. Naturally he would.

He even understood why Susannah had agreed. Where else would she go until the doctor cleared her for travel? She certainly wasn't going to check in to the Bide-A-Wee Motel with a newborn baby.

No one but he and Susannah knew what had passed between them, or ever would know. So he'd smiled and nodded and agreed that of course Susannah and the baby must have the best room at the lodge.

Rhoda and Jen had spent the day before getting the bedroom and attached sitting room ready. He'd managed to stay out of their way, pretending he had work to do. But when he'd run into Rhoda trundling a bassinet down the hall, he'd known he had to get out of the lodge entirely.

Well, he couldn't find any more excuses to keep himself at the office. He had to go home.

Susannah's words kept echoing in his mind. She wouldn't settle for less than his whole heart, and he didn't have that to give. He'd known that from the beginning, and that fact should have kept him from taking a step that had just ended up hurting both of them.

He pulled into his usual parking space. Okay, he could do this. The only consolation was that Susannah would be just as eager to avoid him as he was to avoid her.

He walked into the front hallway, to be nearly knocked over by his father wielding a broom.

"Sorry, son." Daniel smiled. "I guess I'm out of practice with this thing."

"Let me have that before you hurt someone." He took the broom. "Why are you doing this? Isn't sweeping the hall Rhoda's job?"

"Rhoda's busy making up the yellow room."

"Why?" He couldn't help the sharpness of his tone. "Tell me it's not more guests. I thought we agreed the season was over."

"Enid Laine's on her way up from Philadelphia." Daniel looked surprised that he hadn't figured that out for himself. "Sarah Grace is her only grand-child. Naturally she'd come to see her."

Naturally.

"Does she have to stay here?" That was starting to sound petty—he could hear it as soon as the words were out.

"Now, Nathan."

"I know, I know. You could hardly send her somewhere else. How long is she staying?"

"As long as Susannah is here. Then she'll drive back with her and the baby."

He wanted to ask when. He couldn't.

"Susannah thinks the doctor will let them leave the end of the week."

"I see." A few more days. And then he'd never see Susannah again.

Daniel put his hand on Nathan's shoulder, some of the pleasure going out of his face. "I'm sorry, son. I don't know exactly what happened between the two of you, but whatever it was, I'm sorry it turned out badly."

Apparently he wasn't as good at hiding his feelings as he'd thought he was.

"It's all right." He shrugged. "It just wasn't meant to be."

His father reached for the broom. "Now let me have that. I've got work to do."

"You shouldn't," he said automatically.

"Nathan, I'm all right." His father said the words with a sureness he hadn't heard in months. "I'm all right. You can't protect me from living. And living or dying, I know I'm in the Lord's hands. So let it go.''

Nathan held on to the broom for another second, feeling as if he hesitated on the brink of something frightening.

Living or dying, I know I'm in the Lord's hands. That was what Linda had believed, too.

He let go.

Before he could say anything, Jen rushed down the steps carrying a laundry basket.

"I've got to get this in the wash," she said, as serious as if she carried the secret to world peace. "The baby wet all the way through her nightgown and the sheet, and I told Susannah I'd do them right away.''

She whisked past.

He lifted an eyebrow at his father. "Jen, willingly doing laundry?''

Daniel smiled. "Having a baby around the place changes everyone.''

"I guess so.'' *I haven't changed. I can't.* "Guess I'll go get out of this uniform.''

His father's words continued to ring in his mind as he mounted the stairs. Susannah's baby was changing everyone.

Daniel, taking charge of things and acting like the strong, capable man he'd been before the heart attack. Jennifer, turning into a willing, cheerful young woman.

Even Susannah had changed. She was a mother now, and she put her baby before everything else, including her own happiness.

His assessment wasn't fair, and he knew it. He couldn't blame his and Susannah's problems on that little scrap of an infant. The baby had just made the barrier that stood between them clearer.

Susannah couldn't settle for less than his whole heart. He didn't have that to give. It was as simple, and as impossible, as that.

Chapter Fifteen

Nathan had just reached the upstairs hall when he saw Susannah emerge from her room. She'd seen him. It was too late to retreat. All he could do was walk toward her, trying to arrange what he trusted was a normal smile on his lips.

And praying they could avoid talking about what had happened between them.

"Hi. How are you feeling? Glad to be out of the hospital?"

"I'd have to say that Sloane Lodge is a lot more comfortable than that hospital room." She wrapped her arms around herself in an attitude of protection. "And Jen and your father are far more cheerful than any of the hospital staff I met."

He could see tension written in the fine lines around Susannah's eyes, but her natural tone would fool almost anyone. Except him.

"You've certainly revolutionized Jen. She's actually happy about having laundry to do."

Her smile slipped into something a little more natural. "She's a good kid."

"Yes. She is." He hesitated. Maybe now wasn't the time to bring this up, but Susannah had a right to know. "We heard from Jen's mother. Her new husband has business that will keep them away indefinitely, and she doesn't want Jen with them. Oh, she dressed it up better than that, but that's what it amounts to. She has an elderly aunt who'll take Jen in for a while."

Her eyes went wide and dark with pain. "So you're getting what you want, aren't you?"

"I thought so." He really had thought that. "But when it came right down to it, I couldn't do it. So we put the question to Jen, and she wants to stay here. And we want to keep her, as long as she is able to stay."

She seemed to be measuring his reaction. "Is that really true? You really want to keep her?"

Was he sure that was what he wanted? Sometime over the past weeks he'd begun to see Jen differently. Since Susannah had come, as a matter of fact. And the night of homecoming, when Jen had turned to him, had sealed it, even though he hadn't admitted it at the time.

"I think it's the right thing to do."

"Her mother could present an obstacle." Susannah seemed to slip into attorney mode. "You and your father don't really have any legal standing."

"No, but at the moment her mother seems willing enough to have us take Jennifer on. As for the future—well, even if her mother's attitude changes, at least Jen will know she always has a home here."

Susannah's eyes grew bright with tears. "I'm glad. For all of you. Jen needs a family."

Family. Was that really what he was saying? He wanted to protest, but he couldn't.

"Yes, well…" His voice had roughened. "I think maybe Dad needs her as much as she needs him."

"And you," she said. "She needs you, too, Nathan. She relies on you."

He shrugged. "We already know I'm no good with teenage girls, but she seems willing to forgive that."

Was Susannah wondering how he could accept Jen as a family member and still be unable to make the commitment she asked for? He wanted—he still wanted to ask her to stay. He wanted to grab her hands and tell her he'd do anything if only they could make this work between them.

But he couldn't. Some part of his heart had died with Linda and their son. He didn't have enough left to offer Susannah and her baby what they needed.

Susannah seemed to feel that the silence between them was growing awkward. She shifted uneasily, her body newly slim in the loose sweater she wore.

"I guess you've heard Enid is arriving shortly.

I'm sorry to be filling up the lodge again just when you'd gotten it cleared out.''

"Don't think twice about that. I'm glad you're here, and of course Enid would come.''

Susannah's chin rose as if she were forcing herself to say something that she didn't really want to. "About what happened between us—"

"Don't." He couldn't handle talking about it, not now. "I was wrong to say anything about it. We both know that.''

"Not wrong." She made a small gesture with one hand, as if she wanted to reach out to him but had reconsidered. "I'm not sure it's ever wrong to let someone know you care for them. It's just—I'm afraid the timing was never right for us, no matter how much we might wish otherwise.''

"I guess not." He thought about that. If he'd met Susannah years earlier, if she hadn't been married to Trevor, if she hadn't been pregnant…

No. He couldn't say he honestly thought their relationship would have turned out any differently.

He might want to change, but some things were impossible. He didn't know how to do it, and if he tried and failed, Susannah and her baby would be hurt. She wouldn't risk that, and he shouldn't have expected her to.

A thin wail came from the room behind Susannah, and she jerked around as if there were a string attached to her. "The baby. I have to go.''

"Of course." He managed to keep the slight smile on his face until she'd closed the door.

This was for the best, he assured himself again. They both knew that. Unfortunately that didn't seem to make it hurt any less.

Susannah realized she was shaking once she had the door closed between herself and Nathan. She leaned against the sturdy panel, wondering if he still stood there in the hallway, inches away, with that lost look in his eyes. How hard it had been to preserve a serene exterior when all she'd wanted to do was walk into his arms.

No. That door was definitely closed between them, just as the door to the room was. She crossed the room and lifted Sarah from the wicker bassinet. The fretful wail stopped immediately, and Sarah's tiny face turned automatically toward Susannah's breast.

"Greedy little thing," she said softly, her heart aching with love for her child. "Let's get you fed." She went to the rocker and settled into place.

It was amazing how comfortable this business of mothering was already. All the fears she'd had before Sarah's birth had been swept away, replaced with a love so fierce it couldn't be measured.

She stroked the baby's soft dark hair. "I rocked you in this chair before you were even born," she told her daughter gently.

She'd thanked Daniel for bringing the chair up from the cottage, but he'd disclaimed responsibility.

Nathan had brought it. Nathan had set it here, ready for her to rock her baby in. How much pain had that cost him?

Father, I'm trying to look beyond my own hurt and think of Nathan. He desperately needs to break free of the grief and guilt that's paralyzed his heart. Please help him find his way. Let him open his heart so that it can heal at last.

The words of her favorite verse sounded in her mind. "Everyone who loves has been born of God and knows God."

If only Nathan could see that he had love to give. He refused to recognize that fact. He couldn't take the step toward that love.

She'd like to believe there was still a chance for them, but she couldn't. Their chance had come and gone, and there was no going back.

Still, she'd done the right thing, no matter how painful it was. She wouldn't make the same mistake with Nathan that she had with Trevor.

Sarah had fallen asleep in her arms, her rosebud mouth a little open, a trickle of milk on her chin. Susannah wiped it with a gentle finger, smiling when her touch started the baby's mouth moving, even in sleep.

"True devotion," she whispered, dropping a gentle kiss on Sarah's head. "Maybe, someday."

A measure of peace settled in her heart as she rocked her baby in Linda's rocking chair.

Dear friends, let us love one another, for love comes from God.

She'd never regret loving Nathan, even if their love hadn't been meant to be. Loving him had helped her deal with the pain of the discoveries she'd made here. It had made her a better person. She wouldn't regret that. Eventually the pain would fade to a bittersweet memory, and she'd be whole again.

Until then, she had her baby to love and protect. That would be enough.

She heard a clatter in the hallway below, and then a high, excited voice.

Enid. She felt her muscles tense and forced them to relax. Enid was here. She could hardly have avoided calling her, and she couldn't keep Enid from coming once she knew.

But there were painful truths in Lakemont—truths from which Enid had to be protected. Trevor would have done anything to keep his mother from knowing about his father's indiscretions, and she could only hope to do the same. Somehow.

He'd wakened every time the baby cried during the night, and he looked it. Nathan scowled at his face in the mirror. Even a shower and a shave hadn't improved matters.

He'd tried pulling a pillow over his head. That

hadn't helped. Faint though it was, that tiny cry seemed to travel down the hall, creep under the door and wrap itself around his heart. He hadn't known what to do with the emotional response it generated.

He still didn't. Ridiculous, but the feeling wouldn't go away.

He'd go to work. The routine would keep him busy, and another day would tick quickly away once he got into it. He'd be that much closer to the moment when Susannah and her baby would leave for good.

When he reached the hallway he saw that the door to Susannah's sitting room stood open. Without forming the conscious thought in his mind, he started toward it.

This wasn't a good idea. But the compulsion was stronger than his logical mind.

He paused in the doorway, and Susannah looked up from the tiny clothes she was folding and smiled. The shadows under her eyes marred her fair skin. She looked beautiful.

"How are you this morning?" He said the words softly, mindful of the infant who slept peacefully in the bassinet at the far side of the room.

"I'm fine." She nodded toward the bassinet. "Now she's sleeping. She seems to have her days and nights mixed up. I hope she didn't keep you awake last night."

"Not at all." *Liar.*

He took a few steps toward Susannah in spite of

himself. There was so much he wanted to say to her, so much he couldn't say. The unspoken words seemed to hover in the air between them.

"Well, actually I did hear her. She's all right, isn't she?"

"Perfectly." Her smile was possessive, contented. Proud, even. "She's just still at the stage of wanting to eat often. That'll last for a while."

"You sound like a pro."

"I have all the books at home. Of course, Sarah hasn't read them, so she doesn't know what she's supposed to be doing, but I think we'll make out okay together."

Alone together. That was what she was saying. Susannah and her child were embarking on a future that didn't include him.

"I'm sure you're glad to have Enid's help."

"Yes." Her eyes clouded. "I'm happy to have her here, of course. I'm just a little concerned about—well, about the fact that it's *here*."

"Have you told her anything?"

"Not yet. She's been so wrapped up in the baby that she hasn't asked any questions, but I know she will."

She was so determined to protect Enid from knowing the truth. Now that the moment was here, he didn't know how easy she'd find it.

"No one here will want to let the truth slip out," he said carefully. "But maybe you ought to consider—" He stopped, not sure how to go on.

She met his gaze, her eyes startled. "You think I ought to tell her."

"I think it's none of my business."

She wrapped her arms around herself. "That's right. It's not."

He took a step closer, careful not to touch her. "Secrets can be hard to keep, and sometimes keeping them does more harm than good." He was treading on dangerous territory, but he had to say it. "You know that."

"You mean because Trevor kept secrets from me." Pain touched her eyes.

"It hurt you needlessly."

"But that was different. I certainly could have dealt with the truth. It wouldn't have hurt me. Trevor and his father always protected Enid from anything unpleasant. I'm just trying to do what they would have done."

He didn't speak, just looked at her and waited for her to hear the implication of the words she'd said.

Her breath caught. "That's how Trevor saw his father treat his mother his whole life—as a lovely, decorative asset who had to be protected from any unpleasantness." She looked at him, her eyes searching. "And that's how Trevor treated me. That's why he didn't tell me the truth."

He shrugged. "People seem to repeat the patterns they grew up with. Maybe, if he'd had more time, Trevor would have learned how to break that pattern."

"You think I should break it now, don't you?"

I just want you to be happy, Susannah.

"I don't know what you should do. You know Enid better than I ever could. I just think that embarking on a lie now might get to be a pretty heavy burden for you somewhere down the road."

Her face was so troubled that he wished he'd never brought it up. And he wished he could put his arms around her and kiss away all her concerns.

Quick footsteps sounded in the hall behind him, and Enid rushed into the room, the filmy dress she wore fluttering around her like a butterfly's wings. She was already talking, apparently without caring who was there.

"I was just talking with Daniel at breakfast, and I was saying to him that I just don't understand what in the world you were doing here, Susannah."

She caught sight of Nathan then, and paused long enough to give him a gracious smile.

"Not that you and your family didn't take wonderful care of Susannah, because of course you did. But she shouldn't have been here." Her gesture sent her sleeve floating. "She should have been home."

He thought he caught a glimpse of steel through all that fluttering. Enid, he suspected, was going to demand answers, and Susannah would have to come up with some. Whether those answers would be the truth or not—well, that was up to her. He'd said what he'd come to say.

"I'm just on my way down to get some breakfast, so I'll leave you ladies alone."

He shouldn't touch Susannah in front of Enid. He was going to. He took her hand in a quick, reassuring clasp.

Whatever you decide, I'm with you.

That was what he wanted to say, but he didn't have the right to do that. He'd denied himself that right when he'd walked away from her.

But she had to know he supported her. If nothing else, she had to know that.

Susannah curled into the corner of the sitting-room sofa an hour later, feeling as if she'd been shattered and put back together again with a few of the pieces missing. For good or ill, it was done.

Nathan glanced in, hesitated and then came a few steps into the room. "I saw Enid and Rhoda downstairs. They were talking."

She leaned her head back against the sofa, too exhausted to think about getting up. "Yes, I know. Enid said she was going to talk with Rhoda."

"You told Enid the truth, then." He seemed to be measuring its effect on her.

She nodded. "I told her. I wasn't going to, but I kept thinking about what you said. About the harm done by keeping secrets. So I took a breath, said a prayer that I was doing the right thing, and I told her."

"How did she take it?"

Susannah relived that moment in her mind, still not sure she believed what had happened. "She…"

She looked up at Nathan, to find his dark gaze steady on her face.

"You know, I don't think she was even really surprised at some level. Maybe she'd always suspected that her husband wasn't quite the paragon he pretended to be."

He nodded, understanding. "It had to hurt her."

"Yes, of course. But I think she's going to be all right. Enid is a lot stronger than anyone ever gave her credit for. The first thing she said, once she'd grasped it all, was that Rhoda and her son had to be provided for."

She didn't know whether she could have reacted as well as Enid had, if she'd been the wronged wife.

"So that's what she was telling Rhoda. I'm glad I didn't interfere, then."

"Everything seems to be working out for the best." *Except for us, Nathan.*

"It does, doesn't it?" Nathan's face tightened, and she couldn't tell what he was thinking. "My father has Jen to take care of, and Jen has the family she needs. Enid has her grandchild. Rhoda has the comfort of knowing her son will be provided for. Everyone has a happy ending."

We don't. She wanted to throw the words at him. *We don't have a happy ending.*

In a few more days she and the baby would go

away. She'd probably never see Nathan again. Someday that would stop hurting, but not very soon.

There was a rustle of movement from the bassinet, and then a small, fretful whimper. Sarah was probably about ready to eat again.

She tried to smile, but she couldn't quite manage that. "It's about time for me to feed the baby, so…"

So Nathan should leave. So she didn't start to cry in front of him.

Nathan stood for a moment, looking at Susannah. That was his cue to leave. He could walk out and go back to his nice, safe, uninvolved life.

The trouble was that he didn't think he could live that way any longer. But he didn't know if he could change.

You've put limits on the power of love. Everyone else seems able to go beyond those limits. Everyone but you.

The baby's whimpers escalated to a cry. Susannah expected him to flee. It was what he expected of himself. Every nerve in his body seemed to demand that he cut and run. He wasn't strong enough to do anything else.

Instead he walked to the bassinet. He looked down. He really looked, for the first time, at Susannah's baby.

Two tiny fists waved in the air. Sarah's small face was red and crinkled with outrage that her cries were not immediately answered.

He couldn't do this. He had to try.

Please. Show me how.

He bent, scooped up the baby and waited for grief to overwhelm him.

It didn't. All he felt was the most amazing sense of wonder. He held the warm, soft bundle against his chest. Sarah's cries stopped, and she stared up at him with a kind of puzzled frown, as if to ask who he was and what he wanted.

Something seemed to crack open inside him. For an instant it was agonizing. Then, just as suddenly, he felt freedom. Peace.

Just as he'd forced himself to look at Susannah's child, he forced himself to look at his and Linda's baby. His little boy.

For the first time he found he could look at that child with love, not guilt.

He's in Your hands, isn't he?

He knew the answer to that. Gently, sweetly, the lost child who'd haunted his dreams for so long retreated to a corner of his heart. Not gone, but safe there in memory.

Warmth flooded him as he looked at Susannah's baby. Sarah wasn't a memory. She was a living, breathing, demanding human creature who needed him.

He turned to Susannah, wondering how he could possibly find the words to tell her what he felt. His wonderment seemed echoed in her face.

"You know, I think I finally get it." He rocked the baby gently in his arms, and with every breath she seemed to belong there more. "Family isn't about blood. It's about love. God can create a family anywhere, if there's enough love."

Something that might have been hope began to dawn in Susannah's eyes. "Yes." Her voice was very soft. "Is there enough?"

"If you'll forgive me. Be patient with me." His voice went thick with unshed tears. "If I'm lucky, you and Sarah will be my family. And I promise to love and cherish both of you forever."

Susannah held out her arms to him. To them. The joy that filled her face echoed in his heart. He managed to get his arm around her while still cradling Sarah against his chest.

Susannah slid her arms around him, holding him tightly, and turned her face into his shoulder. His arms were full, but not as full as his heart.

They would be a family, created by God. He didn't deserve this happiness, but God had given it to him anyway.

* * * * *

Dear Reader,

I'm so glad you decided to pick up this book, and I
hope my story touched your heart. I loved helping
Nathan and Susannah find their way through life's
tragedies to the love God had for them.

I owe a debt of gratitude to my daughters, Lorie and
Susan, for remind me of what an exciting, frustrating,
wonderful and blessed time pregnancy is!

I hope you'll write and let me know how you liked
this story. Address your letter to me at Steeple Hill
Books, 233 Broadway, Suite 1001, New York, NY
10279,and I'll be happy to send you a signed
bookplate or bookmark. You can visit me on
the Web at www.martaperry.com or e-mail me
at marta@martaperry.com.

Blessings,

Marta Perry

Love Inspired®

THE SWEETEST GIFT

BY

JILLIAN HART

Pilot Sam Gardner was next-door neighbor and a friend to Kirby McKaslin when she needed one…and the man she fell in love with. But Sam was the one who needed Kirby to convince him that, despite his painful past, he could have a wonderful future—with her as his wife!

Don't miss
THE SWEETEST GIFT
On sale March 2004

Available at your favorite retail outlet.

Visit us at www.steeplehill.com

LITSG

Visit Steeple Hill Books online and...

EXPLORE new titles in Online Reads—new romances every month available only online!

LEARN more about the authors behind your favorite Steeple Hill and Love Inspired titles—read interviews and more on the Authors' page.

JOIN our lively discussion groups. Topics include prayer groups, recipes and writers' sessions. You can find them all on the Discussion page.

In today's turbulent world, quality inspirational fiction is especially welcome, and you can rely on Steeple Hill to deliver it in every book.

Steeple
Hill®

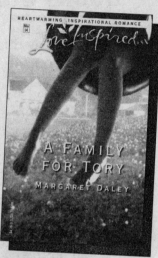

Love Inspired®

A FAMILY FOR TORY

BY

MARGARET DALEY

Victoria Alexander would do anything to help the little girl whose special needs outweighed her own—including marry the child's father! But the pain she'd seen in Slade Donovan's eyes told Tory that his daughter wasn't the only one who needed her. Could God's grace heal all their broken hearts and give Tory the family she'd always longed for?

Don't miss

A FAMILY FOR TORY
On sale March 2004

Available at your favorite retail outlet.

Visit us at www.steeplehill.com

LIAFFT